Th

The Widower

Also by Ray Kluun

Help, I Got My Wife Pregnant

Love Life

Ray Kluun

THE WIDOWER

Translated from the Dutch
by Shaun Whiteside

PAN BOOKS

First published 2008 by Pan Books
an imprint of Pan Macmillan Ltd
Pan Macmillan, 20 New Wharf Road, London N1 9RR
Basingstoke and Oxford
Associated companies throughout the world
www.panmacmillan.com

ISBN 978-0-330-45604-3

Copyright © Ray Kluun 2006
Translation copyright © Macmillan 2008

The right of Ray Kluun to be identified as the
author of this work has been asserted by him in accordance
with the Copyright, Designs and Patents Act 1988.

Originally published in Dutch in 2006 as *De weduwnaar*
by Uitgeverij Podium, Amsterdam

9 8 7 6 5 4 3 2 1

A CIP catalogue record for this book is available from
the British Library.

Typeset by SetSystems Ltd, Saffron Walden, Essex
Printed and bound in the UK by
CPI Mackays, Chatham ME5 8TD

Visit www.panmacmillan.com to read more about all our books
and to buy them. You will also find features, author interviews and
news of any author events, and you can sign up for e-newsletters
so that you're always first to hear about our new releases.

For Eva

Light up, light up
As if you had a choice
Even if you cannot hear my voice
I'll be right beside you dear

Snow Patrol, from 'Run' (*Final Straw*, 2004)

Contents

Prologue

It's eight o'clock in the morning here. I join the waiting queue. We're last off the plane. Everyone's in front of us. Luna is still half asleep, her head on my shoulder. As I carefully shift her from my left arm to my right, I catch a sharp whiff of sweat from my armpit.

After a good half hour we get there.

The interrogation technique used by the Australian official wouldn't be out of place in Germany a few decades ago.

Passport.

'I'm going to have to put you down for a second, darling.' I set my daughter down on the luggage trolley, take out my passport and give it to the official. He starts wearily flicking through it.

This is obviously going to take a while. I poke around in my hand luggage to find a lolly for Luna.

'Tired?'

She nods.

'When we pick up the camper-van you can go back to sleep.'

The official looks at my photograph and turns his surly eye on me. I instantly start feeling guilty. He flicks through to Luna's photograph and looks at me again.

'What's your purpose in coming to Australia?'

Yes, well – hello? If I knew that . . .

'Holiday.'

'How long?'

'A few months.'

How many months?

'Erm – three? Four? Maybe five, if you think that's the right answer.'

Am I making a joke?

Oops, I forgot for a moment: never be offhand with doormen.

'Visa valid for six months. Not a day longer. Understood, mate?'

'Yes. OK.'

'Where are you going?'

'Travelling around. With my daughter.'

'Where to?'

'From north to south, along the coast.'

Can I show him a return ticket? How much money have we got? How will we be travelling? Where are we staying? Where are we spending the first night? Can I show him a voucher for it? The last country we visited?

'Thailand.'

Thailand?!?

Oh-oh. Wrong answer.

Would I read the text here on his little window? It's a list of everything forbidden here. Drink, drugs, weapons, porn, food. The laundry list makes me slightly nervous.

I tell him we have nothing to declare.

Are we bringing any objects out of Thailand? he asks.

'I – erm – I don't think so.'

'Don't think so, or know for certain?'

'I'm sure. I think.'

'No food, then?'

'No.'

'And no fruit?'

'No fruit, either, no.'

'Sure?'

'Yes.'

'So, no food?'

The official looks at Luna, happily sucking away on her lolly.

'Oh.'

Do I know that lying to an immigration officer on duty is a criminal offence?

Red-faced, I take the open bag of lollipops out of my bag and hand it over. The official looks at Luna pointedly. I look at him pleadingly, but he shakes his head.

'Listen, sweetheart, the man says you can't bring the lolly into Australia.' Luna's too tired to protest and just opens her mouth wide. Before she changes her mind, I quickly grab the lollipop and look around to see where I can discard this oh-so-risky item.

The official hasn't had quite enough yet.

Did we visit any zoos in Thailand?

Something inside me says that, judging by what's happened so far, it's probably better to say no.

Will I open my case?

This time something inside me says that no doesn't seem like such a good answer.

The official looks in the suitcase.

What's that sand in my moccasin?

From the beach.

No, can't have sand. No Thai sand in Australia. Tip the sand out. No, not here, over there. And run the moccasin under the tap.

By the time I get back we're the only people in the hall.

The official looks at my passport again. He looks at the stamps in my passport. All my travels with Carmen. He goes on flicking. Ibiza. Bangkok. He looks at Luna.

'Your daughter?'

'Yes.'

He looks in my passport again.

'Where is her mother?'

Christ almighty. That's more than I can take. I look him straight in the eyes and wait for a moment.

'Her mother is dead, sir. She had cancer and died six months ago.'

What happened earlier

You were fucking happy
but it all just came to an end

Jan Wolkers, from *Turkish Delight* (1973)

An elderly man wearing a conspicuous toupee, points to the door with his walking-stick.

'You have got to go in there first, and tell them you're here.'

We get intense and compassionate looks from the other patients. Hospitals have their hierarchies, too. We're clearly new here, we're the waiting-room tourists, and we don't belong here. But the cancer in Carmen's breast has other ideas.

■

I still can't get my head round it. We're thirty-six, we've got a darling of a daughter, we've each got a business, we're living a cool life, we have as many friends as we could possibly want, we do whatever we like, and now we're sitting here on Queensday, the Dutch national holiday, spending half the morning talking about nothing but cancer.

'You could make less of a show of the fact that you're bored,' Carmen snaps at me. 'I can't do anything about the fact that I've got cancer.'

'No, neither can I,' I say furiously.

■

At the supermarket on the Groot Gelderlandplein I look at a man and a woman who must be in their eighties. They're walking arm in arm, shuffling along the wine shelf. I tighten my grip on Luna's hand, and look quickly in the other direction.

The elderly couple, still in love, fill me with jealousy. Carmen and I are never going to do that together.

■

What emerges from underneath the bandage is woman-violatingly ugly. It's the biggest disfigurement that I've ever seen live. A big slit runs across her breast from left to right, about ten or twelve centimetres long.

'It's ugly, isn't it, Dan?'

'It's – not pretty, no.'

I can see in her eyes that she's humiliated. Humiliated by the cancer.

■

'Let me guess. You're having an affair.'

'Yeah. So what?' *OK, give me a full-scale bollocking if you dare, you twat.*

Frank doesn't bollock me.

'I hope Rose is giving you what you need to survive, Danny.'

■

'I don't think I love Carmen any more.'

Rose looks me straight in the eye.

'You do love Carmen,' she says calmly. 'I can tell, from the way you talk about her, the way you let me see her texts. You bring each other love and happiness. You're not happy now, but you do love her. Otherwise you could never do all the things you do for her.'

■

Frank sounds downhearted. 'Carmen just rang. I think you should give her a quick call, or you're going to be in big trouble.'

'What did you say?'

'That I was still asleep and didn't know what time you went out.'

■

'I don't even want to know what you get up to when you're hanging out in the pub till half past four. I don't want to know who's sending you texts, I don't want to know where you are when you don't pick up the phone. I've always suspected that you were unfaithful as a matter of course. If you were ill, I might well do the same myself. I might have started seeing someone else ages ago.'

I look at her, startled. Does she know?

■

'What you're feeling is in fact your liver,' the doctor begins. 'I'm afraid you've got a metastasis.'

Sometimes you hear a word you've never heard before, but you immediately know what it means.

7

'So it's spreading?'

'That's right. It's spreading.'

■

'Mad as it may sound, I'm a bit relieved,' Carmen begins, even before we've left the hospital car park. 'At least we know where we are now. I'm dying.'

All of a sudden she's *joie de vivre* personified.

'I want to go on holiday. As much as possible. Oh, by the way, could you stop for a moment at this snack-bar?'

'Why?'

'Get some cigarettes. I'm going to start smoking again.'

'Ordinary Marlboro or Lights?' I ask her before I get out of the car.

'Ordinary. A bit of lung cancer isn't going to make much difference now, is it?'

■

I sink into my mother-in-law's arms.

'Don't you sometimes wish it was all over?' she asks.

'Yes. If I'm being honest, yes.'

'I understand, too, my son,' she says gently. 'I understand that really well. You've nothing to be ashamed of.'

■

'Danny, you look really stressed,' says Maud. 'Has something happened?'

'No, nothing. Vodka and lime for both of you?'

'I'll have a Breezer,' coos Tasha, putting an arm around me. 'One of the red ones. They make your tongue sweet. You can check it out later, if you like.'

■

Carmen's in the sitting-room, on the Amsterdam home-care bed. With her bald head and her grey dressing-gown on, she gives me a deadly look.

'Where were you when I rang you?'

'With a girl.'

Whack!

For the first time in my life a woman has hit me in the face.

'And as if that isn't bad enough, you drive the car when you're shit-faced!' And then she says it. 'At this rate, Christ knows, Luna isn't just going to lose her mother, she's going to lose her father, too!'

∎

'What's your wife's name?'

'Carmen.'

'Carmen is ready to die.'

A chill runs down my spine . . .

'You don't need to be afraid. She isn't. It's good. I'd go right home now. It's going to happen faster than you think' – BOOM – 'Be sure to be there when it happens' – BOOM – 'She'll be very grateful for it. And so will you.'

∎

Carmen smiles. 'I hope you'll be happy again soon. With a new wife. But you'll have to do something about your infidelity, Danny.'

'Be monogamous . . .'

'No, hardly anyone can do that for their whole lifetime. You certainly can't. But you must never again make a woman feel that she's a complete idiot. That you're shagging half of

9

Amsterdam and Breda, and she's the only one who doesn't know about it. Take care that *no one* knows.'

■

I look guiltily at the floor. I hesitate for a moment, but then decide to ask the question that's been weighing on me. I ask it indirectly.

'Are there still things you want me to tell you? Things you've never dared to ask?'

She smiles again. 'No. You don't need to feel guilty. I know all I want to know.'

'Do you really?'

'Yes. It's fine.'

■

'I want to ask you something,' I say, looking Maud and Frank closely in the eyes. 'I want an honest answer.'

They nod.

'I'm wondering about asking Rose to come to the funeral.'

They're both silent for a moment.

'Do it,' says Frank.

Maud waits for a moment and then nods.

'Yes. I think that would be OK.'

■

'I think I'll wear the Gucci trainers rather than the Pumas,' Carmen says.

'Hm?'

'In the cupboard. With my blue dress.'

■

I lift her up. Her feet just touch the ground. She hangs in my arms, and I turn her round, rocking gently. We're dancing more slowly than we did at our wedding, but we're dancing. Me in my underpants, Carmen in her silk pyjamas. I gently sing the lyrics in her ear.

I want to spend my life with a girl like you – And do all the things that you want me to – I can tell by the way you dress that you're so real fine – And by the way you talk that you're just my kind – Till that time has come and we might live as one – Can I dance with you . . .[*]

When the song is over, I give her a French kiss. It's more intimate than sex.

■

'I love you,' says Luna, suddenly confused.

And then she starts kissing Carmen. Over her whole face. Everywhere. Like she's never done before. Luna kisses Carmen's cheek, her eyes, her forehead, her other cheek.

Luna doesn't say anything. She waves at Carmen, with one hand in mine. And she blows a kiss at Carmen. Carmen holds her hand to her mouth, crying.

Luna and I walk out of the bedroom. Carmen will never see Luna again.

■

The doctor sits with his arms folded, staring out the window.

'Enjoy the rest of your life,' she says gently, and strokes my cheek.

---

*   From 'With a Girl Like You' by the Troggs (1968).

'I will do. And I'll take good care of your daughter.'

'Bye, great love of mine . . .'

'Bye, lovey . . .'

'Here we go, then,' says Carmen. She puts the glass to her mouth and starts drinking.

'Mmmm – this feels good,' she says after a few seconds, as though she's lying in a warm bath. Her eyes are closed.

■

I go out to the garden and tell them that Carmen has passed away. Everyone reacts with resignation. Relieved, without daring to say so.

Frank and Maud just nod.

Thomas stares in front of him. Anne holds his hand tightly.

Luna is cheerful, and giggles as she pinches Carmen's mother's nose.

Her mother, her daughter, their friend, my wife is dead.

Part One

Dan

Don't knock on my door
The door is locked
Let me sleep for a bit
'Cause I'm going insane

Doe Maar, from '1 Nacht Alleen' (*4US*, 1983)

One

Carmen has been lying in the sitting-room for three days now, free of pain, with a contented smile on her face. Admittedly she's looked better, but for a corpse she's certainly not looking too bad.

Maud and Anne put her make-up on the evening after she left us. That's when we first noticed the smile. And, quite weirdly, one of her eyes wasn't completely closed. Like she's winking. At first we all found it a bit macabre, but the more we looked, the more it was Carmen all over. We just left her like that. Even death can't take the fun out of her face.

> ▶ **Maud.** Ex of Dan's, from years ago, in Breda. Now works for MIU, Frank and Dan's business. Over the years she also became one of Carmen's best friends. Can't hold her drink (cool), and certainly can't hold her E (cool²). Quote: 'I don't dare face Carmen any more.'

> ▶ **Anne.** Carmen's best friend, from Maarssen. Dan thinks Anne is Miss Selfridge run to fat. Anne has always thought Dan was just so-so (a selfish jerk who can't keep his hands off other women), but always stood up for him when push came to shove. Quote: 'He's a dick, Carmen, but he loves you.'

The first night I woke up at half past four. It occurred to me then, for the first time, that Carmen would never sleep next to me again. That's when I burst into tears. I ran downstairs, opened the sitting-room door, bent over the coffin and stood there, in my underpants, bawling as I looked at my dead wife in her light-blue Replay dress and Diesel bomber jacket.

The lower half of the coffin is covered with a wooden flap, so you can't see the white Gucci trainers. You can lift the glass plate covering the top half, but I do that as little as possible – which is lucky, because when I was hanging over the coffin on that first night a great big blob of emotion fell right out of my nose. I sorted it out with some window-cleaner and a flannel mitt, and avoided having to get to work with the stain-remover. I don't like the idea of scrubbing away at the dress covering Carmen's stiffened body.

Yesterday, when Luna asked if she could touch Mama, I said no. I didn't think it was great for a child to discover Mama has gone completely cold and stiff. It's concrete evidence that death has set in. Luna looked perplexed. Then I decided to risk it after all. I picked her up and warned her Mama would feel really cold. Luna stuck her little hand out and touched her. She started giggling. 'Mama's like an ice-cream,' she said. Then she asked if she could kiss Mama. OK, now we're getting to it, I thought. I lifted her over the coffin and watched her as she kissed Carm. For Luna, it was the most normal thing in the world. That video of Snow White and the dwarves isn't so weird after all, from an educational point of view.

I'm not quite so cool. I've never been turned off by my wife before, not even when she had her monthly, but right now I find her creepy. My original plan was to place a fresh calla lily inside the coffin every day as long as Carm was laid out here at home, but the first time I did it, it freaked me out. Having to put the lily between her cold, stiffened hands – brrr. And now the smell of calla lilies won't remind me of my gorgeous Carmen in her sexy wedding dress, but of this Carmen, lying here stone-dead in her coffin on stuffed white silk.

■

It'll soon be time for her to go underground. Not that I want rid of her, but my little visits to the sitting-room aren't getting any easier. I go a few times a day, but it's out of an almost compulsive sense of duty rather than anything else. It's like the last night of carnival: you don't feel like it, but you go anyway. You won't have the option later.

If there's someone else there, I feel particularly uneasy. Yesterday, just as I laid the second lily in her hands, Carmen's mother came in. Somehow I got an urge to flaunt my affection for Carm by giving her a kiss. I put my hands on the coffin. Then I hesitated and shivered.

'I hardly dare say it, but the idea of kissing Carmen just makes me feel ill,' I said finally to Carmen's mother.

'That's lucky,' she said with relief. 'I thought I was the only one.'

> ► **Carmen's mother.** Divorced since well into the last century. Knew about Dan's extramarital escapades, but recognized his love of her daughter above all. Quote: 'I'm proud to have you as a son-in-law. And now I want a cup of coffee, you pest.'

This morning we noticed Carmen wasn't just stiff and cold, but she'd also gone a bit purple. I phoned the undertaker and asked if he was absolutely sure the cooling unit under the coffin in the sitting-room was working. That it wasn't set to freeze or something. The undertaker came to inspect his property and assured me Carmen's change in colour was completely normal. Normal, my arse, I thought; it might be your job, but I know what my Carmen looks like when she's not in a good way.

'You're just coming to terms with the idea that her life has really ended, that this really is a corpse. And that's good,' said the man when he saw how worried I was, 'otherwise it would be psychologically impossible for you to bury her tomorrow.'

■

This morning Carmen's mother and I were also shown around the Zorgvlied cemetery. We got a celebrity tour from the lady in charge of our account. I now know exactly which dead Amsterdammers lie where. Near the entrance is the grave of Manfred Langer who used to run the iT gay disco, a bit further along the grave of the children's writer Annie M.G. Schmidt, and even further along you've got the Social Democrat politician Jan Schaefer.

For Carmen we chose a simple plot in the sun, by the path in one of the newer sections of the cemetery.

'She'll like having lots of people walking past,' said Carmen's mother.

'Yes, she always loved pavement cafes. It isn't only old people lying around here, is it?' I asked the cemetery woman.

Our guide had stopped listening ages ago. She took her pen. 'So, that'll be number C3 in section 19–2.'

We nodded. Carmen's arrival always brightened a place, and that's what'll happen here, too, at number C3 in section 19–2.

■

Apart from the first night, I've hardly had time to pine for Carmen. Since she slipped away with that contented expression on her face, I've been working like a dog. Carm wanted her funeral to be a party, and I've always been good at throwing a party, but this was nearly impossible. When you're getting married, you don't arrange the invitations, a location, catering and a DJ three days before, do you?

But anyway it's all sorted. My speech is written, I've laid on a hundred cups of macadamia-nut brittle, there are Liquor-ice Allsorts, there are brownies, the music for the church service has been chosen, and two hundred CDs of *Beautiful Memories* have been burned.

Everyone's looking forward to tomorrow.

And so am I, in fact. After tomorrow my life will start again. Over the past few days I've been able to get used to my new status as a widower. I've been inundated with emails, texts, letters, cards and phone calls. Like I'd climbed the Himalayas with Carmen on my back.

It's really something.

When I was seventeen I spoke German and English, I could nearly drive a car, swim and name all the capital cities in South America. When I was twenty-seven I could drink twenty beers without throwing up, do a bicycle-kick pass to a left-back without breaking my leg, speak to a room of a hundred people without blushing, and pull on a condom without turning on the light. But to learn what love is I had to wait till I was thirty-seven. When my wife developed a fatal illness.

Two

'So I just turn them?'

'Yes.'

'Clockwise?'

'Yes, just like normal screws.'

'I'm not very good at DIY,' I tell the undertaker.

The screws fit the pre-drilled holes of the coffin like they've been made especially for the purpose. I never drilled a hole while our house was being built, but even I can do this. Carmen would be laughing her head off. She always did if I tried my hand at odd jobs.

Dozens of people are waiting downstairs in the kitchen. No one's wearing black, but lots of them are wearing new clothes. Carmen can rest easy. Some of them have just been upstairs to see her one last time. Many preferred to remember Carmen the way she was. That applies to Frank, Thomas, Maud, Anne and Carmen's mother, who will all be carrying the coffin with me. When the undertaker and I have screwed the coffin shut, they'll come upstairs.

> ► **Frank.** Co-owner, with Dan, of the marketing bureau MIU. Straight, but not practising. Not sexually active, or barely. Fashion victim. Best friend of Dan and Carmen. Quote: 'I can't leave you alone on Koninginnedag.'

▶ **Thomas.** Husband of Anne. Old school friend of Dan's from Breda. Nickname: the bear of Maarssen. Not much of a talker. Balding family man, tendency to wandering hands. Quote: 'Not a word to Anne about carnival, OK?'

The death organizer* explains how, standing in two rows of three, we're to lift the coffin, rest it on one shoulder and then hold on to each other's shoulder with one hand and, with the other, hold on to the handle on the side of the coffin. The undertaker looks at us. After pondering for a moment, he changes our positions. He puts Thomas behind Carmen's mother and makes Frank take up his place on the other side of the field, an unusually successful intervention. We have a lot of fun. But our coach still isn't happy and thinks we're probably not up to getting the coffin down the stairs. He has his assistants cover that difficult part of the strategy. Downstairs we take over, and carry the coffin out of the door and into the white hearse.

Everyone is dead silent. There's a bit of sniffling. *Carmen has left the building.*

■

I lift Luna up and put her on my shoulders. She's wearing her little bright-blue dress, the same colour as Mama's. I put two sunflower grips in her hair this morning. She looks heartbreakingly sweet, with her dummy in her mouth. By special dispensation I promised her in bed this morning that she's allowed to keep the dummy in all day long. I also told her today is the day we're going to church with a whole lot

---

* Wrample from *De kleine blonde dood*, Boudewijn Büch (1985).

of people, and we're going to play some of Mama's favourite music, like the song we played at our wedding, and Papa and some other people are going to tell lovely stories about Mama. And after church we're going to drive to the cemetery, where we're going to put Mama's coffin very carefully into a big hole, with lots and lots of sunflowers all around it. She nodded and observed the tear that was trickling down my cheek, but said nothing.

Now, outside, with everyone around us, she's still very quiet. She's holding a soft faceless doll that Anne just gave her, the kind they use at Waldorf schools. I hold on to Luna's legs tightly and stroke her knees with my thumbs. She lays her little hands on mine. I notice most people's eyes are on the little person on my shoulders. The little person who – unlike all the big people – doesn't understand what's going on.

■

The hearse sets off from our house at a walking pace, hatchback open, out into Johannes Verhulststraat, towards the Jacob Obrecht church. I follow it, staring straight at the coffin. I've had two years to prepare myself for this moment, and yet somehow it feels like I'm watching a movie. Like I didn't read the review properly and now I'm forced to watch something I really don't want to see. There in front of me, in the hearse, there she lies, the woman I married six years ago. Carmen van Diepen. I walk behind her in the new white Joop! suit I showed her only last week, her daughter sitting on my shoulders.

So here we are, walking – one in the prime of life, the other with a whole life ahead of her – on the way to his wife's, and her mother's, funeral. I still can't work out what's going on, but if it weren't for the fact I'm going to be the fall-guy, I could almost muster some serious respect for whoever produced this script: hedonist falls in love, gets married, has a child, is unfaithful; wife falls ill and dies; hedonist is left with daughter and a question mark over the meaning of it all. Even I couldn't have come up with that one.

Carmen's mother is walking beside me. She's crying. Behind us a convoy of blubbing friends, colleagues and family. I'm not crying. In some strange way I feel strong as iron. I let go of one of Luna's legs and put an arm around my mother-in-law's shoulder.

Everything will turn out for the best.*

Just watch.

---

*   From *We Beginnen Pas*, De Dijk (2001).

23

Three

'Dear Carmen,

'You wanted to make people think. To tell them they should enjoy each day – your funeral, the rest of their lives, love, friendship, nice clothes, little things, and decadent things. Enjoyment is an art, you said.

'I'll read a little extract from your diary for Luna.

I really hope that I'll leave something behind with people, and they'll tell you about it later. In fact I think, and not just now I'm sick, that if you want something in life you've got to go ahead and do it. You have to enjoy every day, because you don't know all the things that are going to happen later on. Now that sounds like an awful cliché, but it's the only way I can think of putting it.

Once when I was an au pair in London we used to go out a lot to pubs and restaurants. I remember that at one point I had one pair of shoes with holes in the soles. I had no money to get them mended. At least, if it was a choice between new soles on my shoes or a nice evening out with my mates, I opted for the latter. I thought to myself: I'll be happier if I go out and do something nice with other people than if I stay at home on my own with new soles on my shoes.

After that I travelled around the world. I hear about lots of people who wish they'd done the same, but never got round to it. Luna, there are often a hundred reasons not to do something, but just one reason to do it should be enough. It would be very sad if you regretted things you haven't done, because in the end you can only learn from all the things you do.'

I set Carmen's diary down and take a sip of water. The church is deadly quiet.

'Love of my life, I've learned from you and I've enjoyed you.

'I'll miss you, but I'll carry on, however difficult it might sometimes be.

'And I'll take good care of your daughter. Goodbye, lovey.'

Four

The weird thing about Amsterdam is that so much stuff gets nicked, it always comes as a huge surprise to find your bike's still there. I get the same feeling every time I see my little boat exactly where I moored it last time.

It's true today: it's still here. With a calla lily and a sunflower for Carmen and a cool-box with a bottle of rosé, two packs of fruit-flavoured yoghurt and a bag of clown biscuits, I walk over the grass towards the quay. Luna is carrying a drawing she did for Mama this morning. I lift Luna onto the boat, load our supplies and steer the boat via the Apollo Hall basketball stadium and the Okura Hotel, towards the River Amstel and out of the city.

I moor near Zorgvlied. With the flowers and the drawing we walk through the gate with the iron fences and up towards the graves.

■

'It's just a little house now,' says Luna when she catches sight of the sea of flowers by the grave. 'Is Mama's coffin under here now?'

I nod. 'Yes, Mama's coffin is under here.'

'With her body in it?'

I nod.

'At church, people let balloons go into the sky for Mama, didn't they?'

'Yes. Did you think that was nice?'

'Yes. Will they go to heaven?'

'Who knows? What do you think?'

'I think they will,' she says with a serious expression. 'Then Mama can give the angels a balloon. And then they'll all have one!'

'Yes.'

An elderly lady walks past. I quickly wipe my cheeks with my shirt-sleeve.

'Don't be ashamed, this place is full of all our tears,' she says as she walks past the grave.

When I switch my mobile back on and lift Luna back onto the boat, I see I've got five messages. Ramon. Do I fancy going to the Bastille on Friday? Natasha, she's in the Vondelpark with some girlfriends, one of whom Natasha's already told I'm really nice. Frank won't really mind if I don't come into work tomorrow. And Rose?

▶ **Ramon.** Dan's drinking-partner. King of the gym, Emperor of E. Only knew Carmen from parties. Quote: 'Keep infidelity to yourself and your friends.'*

▶ **Natasha.** Also: Tasha or Tash. Trainee with MIU. Young but experienced. Tempted Dan and Maud into a threesome under the influence of Ramon's E. Didn't know Carmen. Quote: 'Feel like a little excitement, Dan?'

---

* Wrample from Hans Teeuwen.

► **Rose**: Had an affair with Dan. Dan texted her to keep her up to date with Carmen's last weeks. Quote: 'Later you'll feel guilty for your whole life, and I'll feel like a slut for the whole of mine.'

> I know you're going to Zorgvlied with
> Luna today. I'm not sure what to do.
> Maybe you need warmth and someone to
> talk to. I just called your au pair, and she
> can look after Luna tonight. Table booked
> at Palma, on the corner near you. My
> treat. X.

I smile. The sweetheart.

Five

'Did someone sleep here last night?' asks the au pair, in English, when I come into the kitchen.

> ▶ **The au pair.** Came to the house when Carmen was ill, with a view to the future. Ugly, vegetarian, sulky. Contrasted nicely with Carmen's love of life, right up to her deathbed. Quote: 'Pfffff . . .'

Luna drops Baby Bunny and runs up to me to give me a kiss.

'Erm – yes.'

'Why?'

'What do you mean, why?'

'Nothing.'

Rose left early this morning. She didn't have to get to work until nine, but she didn't want to run the risk of Luna waking up earlier and seeing her. 'I'll shower at home,' she whispered as she crept into my bedroom from the spare room at seven o'clock. She planted a kiss on my face and tiptoed silently out of the house.

'Listen – I have to go to work. It's a bit late. Can you make Luna a sandwich?'

I tell Luna that I've got to go to work. She looks a little bewildered when I tell her she can play with the au pair today.

I'm still half asleep when I get into the car. Today isn't going to be easy. Frank, Maud and Natasha and everyone will doubtless want to talk about how lovely the funeral was last Friday.

I read on a website about mourning that a lot of people who have lost a loved one benefit from a routine, and that's why I arranged with Frank to come back to work today.

This morning I slightly regret it. It was three-thirty in the morning before I got to bed. What a wonderful evening. Eating pasta with Rose in the evening sun at Palma, and then sitting till closing time at a table outside the King Arthur. We drank another bottle of rosé together on the roof terrace back home, looked at the aeroplanes flying to Schiphol from all directions, and then I had sex for the first time since Carmen's death, on the cushions of the roof-terrace lounger.

I didn't dare go near the bed.

Six

Work doesn't work.

I go in reluctantly every day. I really can't get worked up about whether Holland Casino can penetrate the lucrative market for works outings and group entertainments, or how we're supposed to persuade Volkswagen dealers that the Passat could easily compete with the BMW 3 series if only they believed it themselves.

'Frank, I want a sabbatical.'

'I was afraid of that. What did you have in mind?'

'Um, a – a few months?'

'Starting when?'

'Today?'

'OK, then,' he sighs. 'What will you do?'

'Have a bit of fun. Luna, the boat, read, write, Vondelpark, peace.'

'Yes – mourning takes time, you know,' says Frank solemnly.

'You can say that again,' I reply, pulling out all the stops to make myself look sad. I'm not in the slightest overwhelmed by grief; I just yearn for freedom and tranquillity.

My first period of mourning was when Carmen had cancer.

Seven

It feels like the Summer of Love.

Everyone loves everybody else. Carmen's sickbed and death made us inseparable; we're like a bunch of veterans who fought in the Lebanon together. We're the Survivors.

On Monday evening I cook for Frank and Maud. Actually I can't cook to save my life, but it feels good to do something for them. I rechristen us The Dinner Club,* a splinter movement from the Survivors. The Dinner Club deals with the after-effects of the funeral. Thank-you letters, ordering photographs, that kind of thing.

On other days I often drop in at de Pilsvogel. On Fridays I go out to the Bastille with Ramon, just like I used to, on Saturday there's always a party somewhere and Sunday evening is for Rose. We usually order something from the Thai, or pick up a pizza at Quattro Stagioni on Jacob Obrechtplein, and then we slump in front of the TV.

And Rose is part of it all. Admittedly Carmen's mother doesn't know she exists, but Frank and Maud have accepted her as a member of the Survivors.

---

* Wrample from the title of a book by Saskia Noort.

The bond between the Survivors is getting stronger and stronger.

Maud goes to the gym in the Olympic Stadium with Rose. Carmen's mother spends the evening with Frank, Maud and me in the Pilsvogel, where she's treated like a heroine by Natasha and lots of her friends. At the end of the evening I have to carry her, four sheets to the wind, up the steps to the spare room.

Frank seems to be getting on better and better with Rose. They both love films, and go to the sneak preview at the Criterion together every Tuesday. Maud and Frank go for a weekend in Barcelona together. Maud takes Luna to the zoo. Ramon accompanies Thomas to a motor show in Brussels, and Maud goes with Anne to a musical in the Jaarbeurshal. I haven't actually seen Thomas or Anne since the funeral, but Carmen's mother regularly goes to Maarssen. She takes Luna with her, and when she brings her home afterwards the three of us go to McDonald's or a pancake house.

I'm enjoying myself. For the first time in years, my time is my own.

There are no carping customers, there's no one ringing me in a panic to tell me they're in terrible pain. The only thing that hasn't changed is that I'm still playing mother and father to Luna, just as I did in Carmen's final months, but I don't find it frustrating any more.

I'm proud I've got our home completely under control. I tell everyone things are going fine with Luna. She's affectionate, she talks about Carmen a lot, asks a lot of questions, but I can't see anything that suggests she's very miserable. Mama is dead, that's just how it is. I have the impression the clarity of the situation does her good: Mama isn't there any more, and she has Papa all to herself.

Getting Luna dressed, making breakfast, taking Luna to the crèche, reading her a story and putting her to bed; those are all tasks for Papa, it seems to me. I use the au pair as a sort of posh cleaning lady and baby-sitter. In the evening, when Luna's asleep, I go out. I don't want her to become too dependent on the au pair. In a few months she'll be going back to the Czech Republic, after all.

Tuesday and Thursday are Papa-&-Luna days; on those days Luna can choose what we're going to do. Mostly we go out in our boat or to the playground in the Vondelpark.

Monday, Wednesday and Friday are for me, and Luna's at the crèche, just like before Carmen died.

On those days I sometimes get out an old photograph album: my holidays with Carmen, or her round-the-world trip the year I met her. I still remember how tough I thought she was, a woman going all the way around the world on her own. The photographs of Australia were particularly impressive with a tent in the outback, Carmen with her wonderful body among those ugly aborigines.

I read a lot. Specially stuff about death. Dutch books like *I.M.*,[*] *De kleine blonde dood*,[†] *Turkish Delight*,[‡] And I love the stuff I call 'chairoplane literature'. *The Alchemist*[§] is my favourite, and Frank gave me *The Tibetan Book of the Dead*. You can't get through it, but it looks good on the terrace.

---

[*]   Connie Palmen (1998).
[†]   Boudewijn Büch (1985).
[‡]   Jan Wolkers (1973).
[§]   Paulo Coelho (1994).

34

Spring is fine, in a very un-Dutch way. I spend the whole day sitting in the sun outside the Blauwe Theehuis or the Coffee Company in de Pijp district, reading and writing. In no time I look like I've spent four weeks in the Caribbean.

Apart from father/motherhood, I get most satisfaction from finishing off Carmen's diary for Luna. Every time I want to write about something Carmen didn't get to, I can't help flicking back and reading something she wrote herself. How she met me and how we started going out. How we decided to have a child and ritually threw her last strip of Marvelon pills into the Gulf of Mexico. Our wedding, with our wedding songs, 'With a Girl Like You' and 'Love Is All Around' by the Troggs.

Carmen's diary stories regularly induce me to tears, but weirdly enough that's what I want. That's the benefit of the two years of cancer. Carmen and I learned emotion isn't a dose of flu. Neglect it and a little bit later it'll hit you smack in the chops.

That's why I read the last words of hers that Luna will ever read almost every time. They're on a double-folded sheet of A4. Every now and again when I unfold it, the words, printed in headline-sized letters, leap out at me again.

Most of the time I feel relaly fine, but the mrophine makes me very hazy and I can't rwite and tpye so well. The letters dance on the

srceen and it makes me so tired, darling, that I have to stop again for a momnet. I'll write more later. Tmie for a snooze.

Xxx, mama

I still remember the evening she typed these words, half lying in bed, three cushions behind her back. I could sense how miserable she was that she couldn't write anything more for her daughter, and offered to take over. She shook her head.

'Do it afterwards, when I'm not here any more.'

Afterwards was three days later.

Eight

Natasha is wearing a tight T-shirt with the words BARBIE
IS A SLUT. It comes to just above her pierced navel. She's
wearing blue eye-shadow, and she's got a Kim Wilde curl. The
Eighties are totally fashionable again and I'm joining in for the
second time. Except in those days, thanks to my big fat glasses,
I could never have pulled a girl who looked like Natasha.

'Would you rather the people at MIU didn't know we
were out together?' she asks as we sit outside the Pilsvogel.

'It's a bit awkward. The funeral was only a month ago, if
you know what I mean . . .'

'But shall we have a drink anyway, babes?' she says. She
makes her Bambi eyes a touch more sensual and takes a sip
from her vodka and lime.

'And Rose?' she asks, badgering me. 'Does she know
you're out with me tonight?'

'Rose?' I react testily. 'I don't have to answer to Rose.'

'She was at the church, though, wasn't she?'

I don't answer.

'Come on, Dan, we all know how important Rose was for
you when Carmen was still alive.'

'What do you want me to say?' I reply weakly. 'Rose is a
friend. Not my girlfriend.'

She shrugs.

'That's OK, too,' she says and grabs me by the neck and kisses me full on the lips, outside the Pilsvogel. 'I think it's so looooovely we're sitting here!'

'Yep. Change of subject.' I go and order another vodka and ice and a vodka and lime at the bar.

Tasha has told me she really can't wait to go to The Party next week at the Paradiso.

The Party, I learn from the Pilsvogel barman, is the Old Dutch Acid Party. It sounds like something to do with herrings, but in fact it isn't.

Natasha has already bought a fluorescent Lycra top from Club Wearhouse. 'In Spuistraat, you know the one.'

I nod. No idea.

'You'll be going, too, of course?' she asks. 'Everyone's going.'

▶ **'Everyone'** is Natasha's girlfriends' club. Girls who really could – if Dan put his mind to it in the Eighties – have been his daughters. They look like clones. Like Dolly the Sheep. Anyway they're hot to trot with lots of make-up and are barely distinguishable from each another. Dollies I to V. They all talk the same way, shriek the same way, text the same way, dress the same way, put on their make-up the same way and call each other (and Dan, since recently) darling or babes. Conversations with the Dollies never end, and that suits Dan fine. The first few times he met them it took him a while to get used to their directness, but once he worked out it saved him so much time and hassle, he learned to put up with it. For example, the first time she met Dan, at 2 a.m. in Club NL, Dolly I grabbed him spontaneously by the balls and said she figured it was the quickest way of getting to know someone. He'd already started getting the hang of conventions within the group, so he reinforced their acquaintance with a full-on French kiss. And because the Dollies tell each other everything, everything he did in bed with her that night was public knowledge the following day. *Heat* magazine would die for reporters like the Dollies. To communicate as fast as possible, the Dollies use a kind of text-speak even when they're talking to each other. All words are abbreviated. The Pilsvogel is the Pils, the Chocolat Bar is the Choc, *Odessa* – a boat on the Eastern Quay – is the Boat and the Old Dutch Acid Party is simply called The Party.

'I forgot to get tickets,' I lie.

'I'll sort that out for you, darling! How many do you want? I'll give them a call.' She's already taken her mobile with the Hello Kitty fascia out of her Pippi Longstocking bag, and she's tapping a number in.

'Two. I think Ramon might want to come.'

She lights a cigarette and waits for someone to pick up the phone.

'Not Rose?' she asks, through her nose.

'No,' I say, draining my vodka glass, 'I don't think she's all that keen on house.'

She holds up her index finger. OK, message received.

'Hiiiii, babes! It's meeeee!'

'. . .'

'Ooooooooohhhh, that sounds looooovely. Where are you?'

'. . .'

'Cooool!!! Is that guy with the dyed blond hair from Saturday there, too?' She takes a drag on her cigarette and winks at me. I wink sheepishly back.

'. . .'

'Ooooooh . . . you little slut!' she screeches.

Two women at a nearby table look at us. Tash cranks her volume even higher. I pretend not to be embarrassed, and quickly take a sip.

'Hey, babes, just checking up about The Party.'

'. . .'

'A fluorescent top. And that tarty purple skirt.'

'. . .'

'Oh, great! And those short white pants of yours?'

'. . .'

'Can they really get away with that?'

'. . .'

'What's he say?'

'. . .'

'Heeheehee, listen. What's his name?' She kisses the air at me and runs her hand over my arm.

'. . .'

'Say hi from me. And tell him I'll be in the Choc on Friday.'

'. . .'

'Leave a bit of him for me, darling! Hey, we'll talk again tomorrow. I'm going to hang up now, because I'm here with my boss. Danny, you know, the one whose wife just died.'

'. . .'

I wonder if I should go to the toilet for a minute. I'm about to, but Tash grabs me by the neck.

'Hahaha . . . I'll tell him. But I'm still just a trainee and I think I'd rather get through my ovulat – my evaluation first!'

'. . .'

'Noooooo!'

I tap her on the arm. 'Um – tickets?' I whisper.

'Wait a minute, wait a minute, Dan's saying something to me – what tickets, babes?'

'For that Old Dutch Acid Party you were talking about.'

'Oh, yeah, what a scatterbrain I am. That's what I was

actually ringing about, heeheehee: could you sort out two tickets for The Party?'

'...'

'Yeah, for my boss and a friend of his.'

'...'

'Ok, babes. Thanks. Big kiss. Laterrr!'

She hangs up. 'Where were we?'

I shrug and look at her like I was watching Jaap Stam of Ajax ballet-dancing.

She bursts out laughing again, leans over the table, presses me to her and sticks her tongue deep into my mouth. I taste lime.

'I fancy you tonight,' she whispers hoarsely.

Tasha's directness seems like just what I need tonight.

Not quite like the Eighties, then.

Nine

'Papa!'

'...'

'Pápa!!!'

Christ . . . Pfff . . . Already? I feel as if I've just gone to bed.

'Pááápááá!!!'

How incredibly close that sounds. And what an incredible headache I've got. I'm so dehydrated; all the moisture in my head has been replaced with vodka. Christ alive.

I hear the sound of sobbing. Shit!

I look in the bed beside me. Huh? Oh, yeah. Natasha. There's that, too. She's got to get out of here.

'Tasha!' I whisper. I shake her awake.

'Huh?'

'Luna's awake!'

'Oh – so?' She yawns with a laugh.

'So you've got to get out of here,' I hiss at her. 'I don't want Luna to see anyone in my bed.'

'PÁÁÁPÁÁÁ!!!'

'Wait a minute, darling!' I shout. 'Papa will come and get you.'

'You wait a minute, too,' I order Natasha. 'Get your clothes together and creep down the stairs behind me.'

I quickly hide my morning erection in a pair of boxer shorts, come out of the bedroom and bump into Luna.

She's crying. 'Where were you?'

'Papa was fast asleep,' I answer, and give her a cuddle with my arms round her. She presses her head against my chest. Behind me I hear Natasha tiptoeing quietly downstairs.

'But what's wrong, darling?'

'Bay . . . bee . . . buhuhu . . . nee.'

'What's up with Baby Bunny?' Is that why I had to wake up? What time is it, by the way?

Luna takes my hand and drags me into her bedroom.

There I trip over the army boots of the fat au pair girl with spots, punky hair and a piercing through her upper lip. I'm starting to feel sick.

'Haaaaay,' she yawns. Wearing the inevitable black, over-sized Goth T-shirt and a pair of baggy black trousers, the kind you can only get at the flea-market these days, she's sitting on the activity gym, surrounded by the complete collection of dolls and cuddly toys Luna has assembled over the past few months. Any visiting adult felt a stab of pain to the heart at the idea Luna would grow up without a mother's love. Thank Christ our house is ludicrously big, or I'd have had to build an extra floor for all the soft toys.

Ducky Bill sits in the middle, so it's his birthday today, I can see with my well-trained fatherly eye. I can envision the whole game by now. Bill is surrounded by Furby, Tinky Winky, Little Bas, Big Bas and the anthroposophical doll that Anne gave her and which still hasn't been named, as far as I know. There's a good crowd on the activity gym. Baby Bunny is missing, I see.

Luna starts sobbing again. I see her eye wandering towards

43

the terrifying buttocks of the au pair. There are two little plastic legs sticking out from underneath.

'Why she don't want play no more?' the au pair says crossly, in her special sort of English. She's still learned barely a word of Dutch. Even Luna's vocabulary is bigger than the sulky Czech's.

'Because you're sitting on Baby Bunny.'

'Oh . . .' She pulls the poor doll out from under her bum. One of its legs is broken. Luna's bottom lip starts quivering again.

'Haaay, Baby Bunny, how are you?' says the au pair.

I'd kill for the doll to reply, 'How do you think I am, when you've been sitting on me with your great fat arse?' but there isn't a peep out of Baby Bunny.

Luna starts wailing, and furiously pulls the doll from the au pair's fleshy hands.

'Come on, it's just a doll,' laughs the au pair.

'Baby Bunny was a present from her mother . . .' I say. My eyes spit fire.

I pick Luna up. Oof, not a good plan, after last night. My eyes are a bit hazy. Maybe less to drink next time is a good idea. Luna snuggles into me. 'We were supposed to be doing something nice today, together . . .' she whispers in my ear.

FUCK! She's right. I look at the alarm clock in Luna's bedroom.

10.49.

10.49! Hell! It starts at eleven.

I break out in a sweat.

'Erm – Can you make a sandwich for Luna . . .' I stammer to the au pair. 'I have to hurry . . .'

Ten

A minute later I'm sitting on my bike with Luna, my hangover and two peanut-butter sandwiches, heading for the toddlers' ballet-school test lesson.

As I cycle up the bridge over Prinsengracht, sweating profusely, I tell Luna where we're going. She isn't exactly wild with excitement.

When I explain, gasping, that ballet is a little like the tiny elves who dance on the water-lilies in the Efteling amusement park, and that I've found her a little ballet dress at Hennes & Mauritz ('Oh, yeah, where Mama and I used to buy clothes for me'), she manages a bit of enthusiasm. Lucky that, because if it was up to me, we wouldn't be bothering with all that hopping around today.

As soon as I enter the dressing-room I cheer up a bit. My hangover spontaneously disappears in a flash. Apart from toddlers, there's no one in the ballet-school dressing-room but women. Mothers. And none of your it's-just-another-Thursday-why-should-I-bother-putting-on-make-up sort of mothers; no, these are Amsterdam Mothers. If I'd been told it was a photo-shoot for the new Puma or Diesel summer collection I'd have believed it. All the toddlers have one, a nice Tatum-or-Jennifer mother. I'm the only man. These are the secondary benefits of widowerhood. Yes, I'm going to enjoy toddlers' ballet.

'Morning, ladies,' I say, careful not to get too close. My breath would wipe them all out at the Pilsvogel from here.

I start undressing Luna as routinely as possible, and helping her into her pink ballet dress. Luna is a little embarrassed, I notice. The other children all know each other already, and that doesn't do much for a toddler's self-confidence. That's a shame, because it would be much cooler if Luna could play the part of the self-assured seen-it-all-done-it-all toddler here.

I introduce Luna to the ballet teacher. She's popping out of her ballet dress, it's all I can do to keep my gaze at eye-level.

She tells me the parents are allowed into the hall, if they take their shoes off. I'm familiar with that from the crèche, so I got over that embarrassment years ago.

It's a real ballet hall, the kind you used to see in *Fame* on TV. With a mirrored wall the whole breadth of the hall.

The teacher starts to explain what she's going to do. It's a cloud-dance, she says, and lifts her arms over her head. All the children copy her enthusiastically.

Except Luna.

Again, that's a shame, because as a parent, as a man even, in this circumstance your image depends to a large extent on the happiness of your child. Luna refuses to shift an inch from my side. The ballet teacher explains to her that it'll be really much more fun if she joins in with the other toddlers, but Luna isn't playing.

'I don't want to dance,' she sulks. The sulking turns to tears. The other mothers' attention is now focused on my parenting skills. How is this father going to cope with this crisis?

I get carefully to my feet, showing not a hint of irritation and with a gentle hand and a throbbing headache, lead Luna back to the group. I can feel her trying to drag me in the opposite direction.

'Why doesn't Papa dance, too, then?' I hear myself asking. The teacher nods. Good idea. I'm allowed to join in. Fuck! Luna looks at me. So do eight mothers. Now the gloves are off. I know my daughter well enough to know that if I act as if it's the most normal thing in the world, she will hesitantly follow me. And if I give the merest hint that I don't think the cloud-dance is a normal activity for a thirty-seven-year-old man, she'll drop out, too. Hangover or no hangover, I decide to go for it. Dan the Cloud Fairy.

'Come on, then,' I say in a calm and extremely responsible, teacher voice. I conjure a smile on to my face. 'Do just like Papa does.'

And off Papa goes. Papa looks at the teacher. She instructs us to walk on our toes to the music and at the same time form a cloud with our hands in an O above our heads. And we have to blow, the teacher says. 'The way the wind does.' I can see that. And be careful not to let out a great fart. Out of the corner of my eye I see myself in the mirrored wall. It doesn't look cool. And my face is deathly white.

The group of toddlers plus Papa approaches the Tatum & Jennifer mothers in the corner. I can see they're having fun. I hear quiet giggles. I break out in a sweat. I urgently try and figure out what I can do to keep from looking like a complete dick. Pull a silly face? Wink? Shrug? Blame Luna? Anxiously avoid eye contact? Or just look searchingly around, the way you always do when walking along a terrace cafe when you know everyone's looking at you? Just before I approach the group, on my toes, my arms still held in an O above my head, I quickly make for the toilet door.

■

When I get back, Luna has stopped her cloud-dance again. I notice the teacher is starting to lose patience. She raises her voice. Luna's lip starts quivering. She looks over at me. Super! Let's get out of here. I gesture to her to come towards me, make an apologetic gesture towards the teacher, wave at the still-giggling mothers and quickly leave the ballet hall with Luna.

'Shall we go to the playground in the Vondelpark?' I ask when we're outside.

Luna nods. 'Feed the ducks.'

■

I park my bike against the restaurant fence. There's a poster up. The Tröckener Kecks are giving a concert in the open-air theatre on Sunday. Hey, that might be a good opportunity to meet up with Thomas and Anne. And we wouldn't have to talk too much. Apart from missing Carmen, we haven't actually got all that much in common, so going to see them in Maarssen hasn't been top of my list of priorities for the past few weeks. But I need to keep the bond with them alive. I think it has something to do with the fact that they were part of my life with Carmen. Not that we saw each other too often in recent years. My bond with Thomas has grown weaker and weaker. It was Anne and Carmen who kept it all going. Maybe that's why I don't want to let it fade away.

48

An unconscious homage to Carmen, to the energy that she always put into her friendships?

So I can put my mind at rest about Frank. At the Dinner Club on Monday he hinted he thinks I'm losing myself in Natasha's club with the Dollies, and that I'm neglecting our friendship. Nonsense, of course, because I see him and Maud every Monday, but still.

Yeah. I'll email Thomas later on.

After an hour going from slide to swing to climbing frame to seesaw to sandpit to slide to swing to climbing frame to seesaw to sandpit, my headache has more or less evaporated. We go into the cafeteria. I have a Coke. Luna wants a treasure-chest. It's a new thing from Ola, the ice-cream makers. A blue plastic box with ice-cream in it and a double bottom. When you take it out, you can take out a doll with your sticky strawberry fingers.

'Look, it's just like Mama in her coffin,' Luna says brightly when she sees the doll lying in there. I can laugh. We go and sit on a bench. Luna's legs rock back and forth as she licks her ice-cream. Within seconds she's covered in it. I look in my bag for something to wash Luna's hands with, and plunge my fingers into what's left of the peanut-butter sandwich.

'Shall we go and feed the duckies?' I ask Luna, as I lick my fingers clean.

The duckies immediately come swimming, flying and running over, great flocks of them. Luna jumps up and down with delight as I hand her the bits of peanut butter and bread. Why bother about the toddler ballet? Let's just feed the ducks.

Eleven

From: M.vanduin@yahoo.com
Sent: 26 June 2001
To: Danvandiepen@hotmail.com

Hi Dan,

I don't know if you remember who I am, but I was in Carmen's breast-cancer discussion group.

It was called the Moufflon, wasn't it? No idea who this is.

I wasn't at the funeral, because I can't cope with them, you might understand that. Carmen probably told you about me, we were really good friends in the group.

As far as I knew, the woman Carmen was closest to was Toos. But it can't be her, because she's dead. Half of the Moufflon group is probably dead by now.

What I'm really emailing you about: I'd love to be able to call in and see you some time. Ideally in the day, when Luna's there, too. You'll probably understand that I'd like to see with my own eyes that she's being properly brought up now that Carmen's no longer with us?;) Tell me when it would suit you.

Lots of love,

Marieke van Duin

Well, let me tell you when would suit me, Marieke van Duin. Never would suit me. Now kindly fuck off. Who's next?

> **From:** Neildiamondfan@tiscali.nl
> **Sent:** 27 June 2001
> **To:** Danvandiepen@hotmail.com

Hi my little pest

How are you, son? I'm not so great at the moment. I was fine for the first few weeks, but for the past few days I've just been walking around crying. How's my grandchild? You won't leave Luna with that foreign au pair of yours too much, will you? I don't trust her an inch. She'll end up sitting on the child.

All love,

Your mother-in-law

Sigh. And the next one.

> **From:** Anne_and_thomas_and_the_children@chello.nl
> **Sent:** 27 June 2001
> **To:** Danvandiepen@hotmail.com
> **Re:** Kecks in the Vondelpark

Hey Dan!

What a great idea, going to see the Kecks together. We're in! What time does it start on Sunday? Should we call by at yours first? It's great to hear from you. I've tried to call you, but I only ever get your voicemail. I was saying to Thomas yesterday: we haven't heard from him for ages, that Dan's completely wrapped up in Amsterdam, We've had our ups and downs. I miss Carmen terribly. Thomas doesn't talk about her that much. And what about you? It must be hard. Frank told me you gave up work? Is that OK, with your finances and everything? And how's Luna??? It was great to see her again on Sunday. I think I could give you a bit of MA every now and again (= motherly advice, brilliant, isn't it?).

So, till Sunday!

Love, Anne

MA. Yeah, good one. Christ alive! What are you all thinking? Of course I take care of my daughter, for God's sake. If it was up to you, the child would be pampered to bits. Luna can sit on your lap. Luna can have an ice-cream from the freezer. Luna can have a story for three-quarters of an hour. Luna can stay up when Papa has just told Luna she has to go to bed.

Papa is advised how to get Luna to try food when she complains she doesn't like her beans. Papa is advised he should think about taking Luna to the doctor when she coughs a couple of times. Papa is advised it would be better for Luna if she played more with other children. Papa is advised it isn't good for Luna if he tells her at bedtime he's going out for a couple of beers later and the au pair will be looking after her. And now Papa is also being informed by a couple of surrogate mums that he's doing it all wrong?

What do you lot imagine? That in the two years of cancer, after all the times Carmen had to admit, with tears in her eyes, that she was too weak, sick and ill to look after Luna, that I still don't know how to give Luna a bath and put her to bed, how to read to her, how to cut her toe-nails, how to give her bread, fruit, meat, vegetables, pasta, potatoes, milk and porridge and change her nappy? Who do you think did all that when Carmen was ill? Fucking Postman Pat and his pals?

Has it really never passed through your stupid great heads that this Papa has been to more children's hairdressers, little friends' houses, crèches, goat-farms, playgrounds, Santa's Grottoes, toy, clothes and shoe-shops, advice bureaux, GPs and all that stuff than all your husbands, the fathers of your own children, put together?

And while we're at it: if I hadn't been a single father, but a single mother, would you have had the guts to meddle with Luna's upbringing? Would you?

Papa thinks Luna should know how things stand now that she hasn't got a Mama: there's only one boss in this house and that's Papa, and Papa is getting sick up to the eyeballs of all the meddling cows who are forever giving him advice about Luna's upbringing.

No, Luna hasn't got a Mama any more, but Luna does have a Papa, who she can always rely on, throughout the whole of her life, a Papa who loves her to tiny bits, and she loves him, so fuck off with your know-all advice, deal with your own children, and if you haven't got any, then make a few, but for God's sake

leave me and my daughter in peace!!!

Twelve

'Have you got a dryer in the house, babes?'

Yawn. 'Have I got a what in the house?'

'A hairdryer. You know, for your hair.'

'No, of course not.' I think for a second. 'Although hang on a second – I think there's one in the bathroom. Use that.'

Rose left hers here yesterday afternoon, because she slept here again last night. So I'd better make sure the Dolly takes all her stuff away. I don't want to start rowing with Rose.

The sheep walks back into the bedroom in the nude. She's found the hairdryer.

'Christ,' I say, 'my head feels like I've got a brain tumour.'

'Yeah, that's the downside with that stuff,' laughs the Dolly. She looks at me in the mirror as she dries her hair. One tough cookie. Twenty-three. To think I can do this kind of thing at my age.

I was euphoric last night.

Why had it never occurred to me before? Like the stuff hadn't been sitting on the reserve bench my whole life, patiently waiting to come on to the field, until last night, when Coach Tasha held up the substitute card at the Old Dutch Acid Party.

Ecstasy out, coke in.

Like exchanging an attacking midfielder for a deep striker in a footy match.

Of course I didn't let on I was nervous when I took my first snort in the corner of the balcony.

'So, how is it?' asked Tash, eyes bright, a quarter of an hour later.

'Like my brain's having an orgasm,' I replied, befuddled.

'Wait till you really do have an orgasm,' Dolly whispered hoarsely in my ear.

She was right: the sex from another planet. They ate me up. And each other. And I ate them up. A super-threesome.

Three hours later I'm still lying staring at the ceiling. I remember seeing the radio-alarm clock turning twelve. I must have slept two hours, tops.

I watch her body from the bed. In spite of my headache I'm feeling incredibly randy again. What an arse the kid has . . .

Dolly sees me looking and shakes her head with a laugh. 'No, no, darling. I'm off. Tasha's gone, too. And shouldn't you be heading out too?'

'What time is it, then?' I yawn.

'A quarter to three.'

'Oh.' I think the Kecks start playing at four.

'By the way, your au pair said . . .'

'You've seen my au pair?'

'Yes. I bumped into her last night on my way to the toilet.'

OK. 'And Luna?'

'Who's Luna?'

'My daughter, honey.'

'Yes. She saw me, too. Sweet kid, by the way.'

'Did she think it was, erm – strange you were walking about the place?'

'I don't know. I don't know much about children. But she knows Tasha, doesn't she?'

'Luna saw Natasha as well?'

'Yes.'

'Jesus . . .'

She looks at me blankly and shrugs. 'So I was supposed to pass on a message from the au pair that the friends you'd arranged to meet – what were they called again . . .'

'Thomas and Anne.'

'Yes. That Luna's already gone to the Vondelpark with Tom and Annie.'

Not so bad. Plenty of time. I see the trousers of my Joop! suit lying on the floor in the corner of the bedroom. I promised Carmen I'd wear it at parties. At any rate, I've kept my promise about something. I won't be able to wear it much more often, though, because there's a wine stain on the jacket and the trouser-legs are covered with mud up to the knees. I empty my pockets. Two crumpled hundred-euro notes and a cigarette packet. Hmm. I thought there was more in there. Thank God I've still got my mobile. Always a stroke of luck after a night like that. Let's have a look. Two missed calls, three texts. How popular we are. The first call was from Thomas, the second from Rose. All three texts, too. Shit. Was I supposed to meet her last night?

> Can't get hold of you. Tried to before.
> Lovely weather for sitting outside.

I'm here already . . . White beer and
yoghurt. Kecks are playing in the V'Park
this evening, did you know?

Where are you now? :-(

I gesture to the Dolly to switch off the hairdryer and phone Rose.

'Hi – yeah, I've just woken up and I see that . . .'

'. . .'

'I had a couple of beers and things got a bit out of hand.'

'. . .'

'With Ramon.'

The Dolly stands laughing with her hand over her mouth and wags an admonishing finger.

'Yes. Fine. I'll just shower and then I'll be there. Ten minutes.'

I hang up.

'Ohhohh, Dan,' splutters the Dolly. 'Is that the girl who owns the hairdryer?'

'Yes.' I start picking up bedclothes. 'Could you give me a hand?'

She gets dressed and takes the pillows out of their cases. 'So who is this girl? Why are you lying to her? Everyone knows what you get up to.'

I shrug.

She shakes her head. 'So,' she says, handing me the pillowcases. 'I've got to go.' She kisses me on the mouth. 'Natasha borrowed another few grams of nose-candy from you, I was to let you know. Oh, and I'd brush your teeth before you see your girlfriend. And Tim and Annie.'

'Thomas and Anne. And she's not my girlfriend.'

'And I'd wash that before you see her.' She taps my limp dick. 'You smell of sluts.'

'Sluts?' I ask with surprise.

'Yes. That's what you called us last night.' I sense some displeasure. 'No problem,' she goes on, 'but the biggest slut in Amsterdam is you, Danny.'

Thirteen

'So – slept in?' Rose asks scornfully. She looks wonderful in her summer dress.

'Yeah. Bit of a hangover. Sorry I'm a bit late.' I kiss her, anxiously keeping my lips tightly closed. My hand slides over the thin material covering her bum down to feel her blue thong. She pushes my hand away.

'Your beer's warm.' She looks around and points to a bottle of drinking-yoghurt. 'Isn't Luna here?'

'I was about to say. She's with Thomas and Anne.'

'Who are Thomas and Anne?'

'Friends of mine, I arranged to meet them this afternoon. Didn't I tell you?'

'No.'

'Oh. OK. Well, Thomas and Anne are at the open-air theatre, with Luna.'

'So?'

'So I'm on my way there and then, erm . . .'

'And I'm supposed to sit here till you're finished with Thomas and Anne.'

'Well, no, you can come along, too, but – it might look a little, ah – couply, if you know what I mean.'

'No.'

'Look, if you stay here for just a little while longer, or take a bit of a walk, and then you show up after that, might that be an idea?'

'Great,' she snaps. 'I was invisible before Carmen died, so nothing's really changed, has it?'

Fourteen

The bear of Maarssen is eating a cornetto.

He's wearing one of those inevitable striped polo-shirts of his. And shorts. Anne stands out against the hip, alternative-crowd surrounding. She's wearing the kind of T-shirt I'm not sure you can still get in Amsterdam. In Maarssen it doesn't seem to be a problem.

It's twenty-eight degrees, I see by the thermometer on the side of the Blikkenbar. Try not to let it show. Last week's vodka hangover is nothing compared to this monster. That should sort it out. A moment ago I sneaked into the portable toilet at the open-air theatre for a bit of marching powder. Just this once can't hurt.

Luna sees me first.

'Papa!!!'

'Sunshine!'

She jumps up and throws her arms around me, and hangs from my neck with all her weight. Ow. My head. Dizzy.

I laugh and give her a great big hug. Out of the corner of my eye I see Anne looking at us. A lovely tableau of father and daughter. Hang on in there, in spite of the hangover. So. I set Luna down, spread out my arms and display my widest welcome grin.

'Danny boy!' calls Thomas. He hugs me and slaps me hard on the shoulder.

'Hey, fat guy! Good to see you!'

'Hi, Dan,' says Anne with a smile when I've wriggled out of his clutches. She kisses me three times. Not on my mouth, please not on my mouth. 'Luna was asking where you were.'

'Hey, girl, looking good. Luna, do you want Papa to get you an ice-cream?' You see, the stuff's starting to work. I'm already a bit sharper.

'She's just had one.' Anne strokes Luna's head. She says she's just covered her with sun-tan lotion. She shows me the tube.

'I don't know if it's any use to you,' she says, 'but it's on offer this week. Free bit of MA.' She winks at me.

The sound of cheering and whistling comes from over by the stand. Rick de Leeuw comes out on stage. Anne says that before they came to our house they popped over to Zorgvlied and Carmen's grave was looking lovely.

I stand on my tiptoes. The Kecks are really rocking.

'I was planning to go over tomorrow,' I shout over the din.

Anne tries to say something else, but I gesture I can't hear her.

Thomas yells along with the words of the opening number.

'I go out – every night – every night in town – every night till early morning – and I drink – I drink every night – drink too much every night over you – too much but never enough – because I want more more more – more than I can have – more, more, more – more than I can have…'

He moves his impressive torso around so violently he

looks like archive footage of Europe's 1986 'Countdown Live' concert. The top of his balding head glistens with sweat.

The audience cheers when the song is over. Thomas whistles on his fingers. His polo-shirt is just as drenched as Rick de Leeuw's pink shirt. Anne asks how I am.

'Good!' I say, a little too abruptly. She raises an eyebrow.

'Shhhhtt,' says Thomas. 'I like this one.'

Rick sings quietly, his eyes shut.

'*I never think of you – When I wake up in the morning, beside a woman I don't know – I never think of you.*' I sob quietly. '*When I walk into the pub we always used to go to, I never think of you…*' Anne looks at me and throws her arm around me. I put my arm round her waist. I feel tears welling up. '*No, I never think of you…*' Anne rubs my back with her hand. '*Never think of you – no, I never think – I never think – I never think of you.*' Tears run down my face. Anne kisses me on the cheek. Thomas stands there awkwardly.

'Shall we go forward a bit?' he yells, when the song is over.

I wipe my tears away and shake my head. 'A girlfriend of mine might be coming,' I say, as casually as possible.

'Oh, that'll be nice,' says Anne. 'Do I know her? Someone we saw at the funeral?'

I think for a moment. It's possible they did see Rose, and they might recognize her. I lift Luna up and put her on my shoulders to gain some time.

Thomas is standing in front of me. 'I hope it's the girl from work, the one with the – Russian name?' he asks eagerly.

'The one who wore the crop-top at the funeral,' Anne adds.

'Natasha. No, not her,' I say. 'I don't think you know her. Someone I, erm – know from the Pilsvogel. Her name is Rose.'

'Oh,' says Anne. She turns her face towards the stage.

'I bet you've given her one, haven't you?' asks Thomas in a low voice.

'I heard that,' snaps Anne. 'Ugh, how disgusting. Dan wouldn't dream of doing such a thing.'

That's the great thing about Thomas and Anne: you're saved by the bell after every awkward question. Just keep your mouth shut and wait till one of them corrects the other with a marital snarl.

Rose comes running over.

I wave.

'Is that Rose?' Thomas yells in my ear from behind. I nod. 'Nice mini-skirt.' His tongue is nearly hanging out of his mouth.

Anne shakes Rose's hand, Thomas gives her a hug, his thumbs feeling the sides of her breasts – not knowing Thomas very well, she'll give him the benefit of the doubt, and put the positioning of his thumbs down to chance. 'Don't I know you from somewhere?' he asks, digging around conspicuously in his memory.

Shit! Last year. Carnival. De Bommel. Rose looks at me anxiously.

'I'm sure you don't,' I leap in. 'Now that everyone's here, we could go up to the front. Would you like that, Luna?' She nods.

'Hi, Luna,' says Rose.

'Hi...' says Luna, in a barely audible voice. Today I consider myself lucky my daughter's so shy. It's like she's seeing this lady for the first time, rather than twice in the past week.

Anne asks Rose what she does for a living ('account manager at a small advertising agency'), whether she likes it ('not really, a bit superficial'), how long she's been working there ('six months, I was working as a marketing manager for a travel firm, but I wanted to work in Amsterdam') and – I was already thinking, when are we going to get there – where she knows me from ('the Pilsvogel,' I answer quickly).

Rose asks if we'd all fancy some wine. Before her face has the chance to turn bright red, she's already pushing her way through the crowd to the bar.

When she's back with a bottle of rosé and four glasses, we wriggle our way towards the stage. It isn't easy for Thomas, all sixteen and a half stone of him. I see rolls of fat under his arms.

'Pff, too many people here,' says Anne. She irritably shoves aside a boy who's standing in her way.

'Shall we just stay where we are?' asks Thomas.

Out of the corner of my eye I see good reasons why that's a very bad idea. I quickly fetch Luna, who is towering above the crowd like a flag, down from my shoulders.

'Oohoo . . . Darling!'

Too late.

Natasha comes running over with three Dollies in her wake, including the one from this morning. Before I can get a fix on what's going on, Natasha has thrown her arms around my neck and is greeting me as if we hadn't seen each other for years. She takes my face in her hands and kisses me full on the mouth, right in front of Rose, Thomas, Anne and Luna.

Hello to you, too.

She's wearing a tight black cap-sleeve T-shirt. Too short, of course. It bears the word LOVE in big glittering letters at bosom-height. I see Thomas gazing alternately at the letters and the navel-pierced belly. Last night's Dolly hugs me again, so fervently that her breasts are only a couple of inches from my face, just as they were a few hours ago, only this time they're wrapped up. She has changed and put on make-up at home. Green eye-shadow, a family pack of lip-gloss, a tartan mini-skirt and an army-green sleeveless T-shirt with a print of Che Guevara.

I wouldn't rule out the possibility she thinks he's a pop-singer.

Luna's clearly surprised to be suddenly surrounded by so many people that she's recently seen walking along our landing at home, albeit with no clothes on. She looks open-mouthed at Natasha and the Dolly she recognizes. I introduce everyone. Thomas immediately seizes his chance and kisses all three Dollies, grabbing them with his big hands. There's no escape. Anne glares with disapproval and gives all the Dollies a firm handshake.

'And – then you must be Rose?' coos Natasha.

'And you are – ?' asks Rose. I sense a certain coolness.

Natasha doesn't.

'Oohoo, Rose, at long last I get to see you!' Unabashed, she grabs Rose around the waist and kisses her full on the mouth, just as she did to me a moment ago. 'How loooooov-ely you're here too!!!' I feel like I've landed in a Ray Cooney farce. One tiny little reference from one of the girls to what happened this morning and I'll have a heart attack. And so will Rose and Anne.

'Darling,' coos Natasha to last night's Dolly, 'this is Rose! You know the one!'

Yes, she knows, OK. The Dolly winks at me.

'What a shame you didn't want tickets for yesterday's Acid Party,' Natasha goes on. 'It'd have been nice for us all to get trashed together.'

Rose says she has to go to the toilet.

Luna tugs at my sleeve.

Anne tells Thomas she wants to go home, it's getting late.

Fifteen

I walk with Rose towards the park exit near the Vondelkerk. 'Why didn't you want me there yesterday?' she snaps.

'So am I not allowed to do anything without you?'

'In that case, why don't you just say you want to go without me? Did you desperately need to f—?' She looks up at Luna, sitting on my shoulders, and falls silent.

'And why not? You're not my girlfriend.'

'Oh, don't I know it! You know what you can do? You can screw the whole of Amsterdam if you think it'll make you happy!' she yells furiously.

'Rose, come on –' Embarrassed, I look around me. Luna's weight on my head tells me she's fallen asleep. Rose doesn't care.

'You know what? Why don't you just go on shagging those Dolly the Sheep girls of yours!'

Then she turns round and walks straight out of the park.

I wait for a moment until she's out of sight and then take the same exit. I don't want to walk back along the Vertigo terrace again.

A little while later I hear a message alert.

**I'm not coming tonight. If I can't have
your warmth, I don't want your coldness
either.**

I quickly delete the message and walk out into Vondelstraat.
When I'm on the corner of the Overtoom and Constantijn
Huygensstraat, the Line 3 is just pulling up. I fetch Luna
down from my shoulders and carry her on my arm into the
tram. I carefully set her down on the seat next to me.

'Pap, I'm tired . . .'

Oh, yeah, now you start. 'Just go to sleep, lovey.'

When the tram gets going, my phone rings. Not Rose, but
the Dolly from last night.

'Hi, babes – did you have a row?'

The tram crosses the Vondelpark Bridge. I say nothing.

She giggles. 'Hey, do you fancy going to Bloemendaal
with us? We're in the car already.'

'Well, I was really planning to go home.' Hmm – messing
around with the Dollies in the sand – 'Where?'

'De Republiek. Shall we pick you up at home?'

'No, I, erm – wait a second . . .' The tram stops at Conser-
vatorium. I get up and push my way between the people to
get out. 'OK. Pick me up at the corner of Willemsparkweg
and Van Baerlestraat.'

'OK, darling. See you then!'

I put my phone away. Glad I'm off that sticky tram. All
of a sudden a shock of horror runs through my heart. The
Line 3 slowly pulls away. My eyes flit along the windows of
the various carriages.

Suddenly I see her. She's kneeling, her face pressed in
panic against the pane.

Through the glass I see her mouth forming a soundless cry of terror.

'Paaa-paaa!!!'

I'll take good care of your daughter. I start running along the tram-rails down Van Baerlestraat behind Line 3.

I catch up with it at Concertgebouw, thank God.

Sixteen

Halfway through July, two months after Carmen's death, I look at my diary and see I've spent a total of four evenings alone.

My new discovery leaves me bursting with energy. I can get by with an average of about four hours' sleep.

Rose knows nothing about it. Apart from half a tablet once or twice a year she stays away from drugs. Last year she had her first party at the ad agency where she now works, and they use tons of the stuff, she told me.

'It didn't make anyone any nicer that evening.' Wisely I keep my mouth shut. Where drugs are concerned, Rose could have been Carmen's sister.

I've decided not to mention anything at all about the Dollies and related matters. Rose and the Dollies are never going to mix. And that's OK, because I don't expect them to be all that close. And it's better that way. On Sunday morning, when I wake up after a heavy night out with Ramon or the Dollies, I look forward to spending the evening at home, cuddling with Rose on the sofa. *Cold Feet*, wine, toast. It balances the weekend out nicely.

And I'm anxiously on the lookout for any signs Rose might get the feeling we're boyfriend and girlfriend. I do like to pamper her. Sometimes I set aside the whole of Saturday and Sunday for her, and we go to Antwerp or Rotterdam. Last weekend I asked Anne and Thomas if Luna could stay with them for the weekend, and we went to Paris together. No one knew about it, not even Frank and Maud. Then you have to explain everything all over again, and I don't feel like it.

After an intimate evening or weekend with Rose I've had enough of cuddling. I notice I start getting peevish and have to be careful not to be too conspicuous about texting to arrange something for the following day, with Ramon, Tasha or one of the Dollies.

Coke forges a bond, however you look at it. It makes everything so convivial.

Seventeen

No one escapes the Summer of Love.

Even Ramon steps into the sweet-shop. First he has Natasha, then, systematically, one Dolly after the other and, to complete the circle, Maud. Just like me. Every Monday evening, after the Dinner Club, she stays behind when Frank goes home, and we do a spot of blow.

At the age of thirty-four, Maud herself has discovered an unsuspected interest in the female body. Tash initiated her, along with one of the Dollies. Even Frank has picked up the Summer of Love feeling, and went home with a Dolly after a party in More. In her grave, if she has room, Carmen would be slapping her knees with joy.

I'm the pivot of it all. The widower. Some days I'm like Billy Smart's Circus, three shows a day.[*] I minutely record all the formations, scores and substitutions in my diary, like Louis van Gaal, the former Ajax manager. At the back, under the heading 'to do', are the names of players I still have on my wish-list. Whenever I look into it again after a few weeks, I'm able to tick off another two or three.

---

[*]   Freely wrampled from *The Shadow of the Wind*, Carlos Ruiz Zafón (2004).

Rose is the top scorer, closely followed by Maud. With Tasha I'm on an average of once every two weeks, quite an achievement given all her other activities. And then there are the regular Dolly substitutions, and now and again a fresh catch of the day.

Paradiso, the Pilsvogel and More are particularly well-stocked fishponds, but I've even had a bite on the terrace of the Coffee Company in de Pijp, at eleven o'clock in the morning. Like it's written on my face or something. Before lunch we're shagging in her student room three floors up overlooking the Sarphatipark. An hour later I'm back in the sun with a latte, reading *The Alchemist*.

Ramon introduces the term wheelbarrow shagging, or network sex. I help him to the Dollies. He pays me back with a female colleague of his who lost her husband to cancer two years ago. Do I fancy having a chat with her? 'And she's a looker, too.' He's right.

I've known Thomas's sister for ages, I hadn't seen her for years until Carmen's funeral. With a whisper I get her phone number from Thomas, and send her a text asking if she fancies going out one evening soon. For form's sake I wait a few weeks before phoning her. That same evening she comes over and, well, comes.

The Dollies are the best wheelbarrows. The girls from their circuit offer themselves up on a plate in the pub ('Hi, you're Danny, aren't you? I heard from Tasha that you—') or by text ('I got your number from a friend who told me that you'd really like to . . .').

Widowerhood works, in short, like a magnet. It brings out women's natural need to care, to comfort and to be nice.

When I'm chatting people up, I bring up the subject of my wife's death right at the start.

'How come you haven't been out for so long?'

'You don't want to know.'

'No, tell me.'

'Yeah, but we're having a nice time, and then I'm going to spoil it all for you with horrible stor—'

'What happened?'

'OK. My wife recently died of cancer.'

No one refuses a widower anything.

If the left-hand approach doesn't work, then come in from the right. I'm as persuasive as a photocopying-machine salesman. If my widowerhood isn't a convincing sales pitch, then I'll throw in my huge house in Oud Zuid. An infallible pitch, particularly with career girls. The younger girls who get wheelbarrowed back to my place via the Dollies are more interested in the short-term advantages – coke and a credit card after dinner.

And if I don't want to take any risks at all, I throw in Luna. Then I just invite one of my to-dos to our house and show what a good Papa I'm not.

'Listen, darling, will you wait for a moment while I read to Luna and put her to bed?'

'Doesn't your au pair do that?'

'No, because she's my daughter.'

It's like the greenhouse effect and the icecaps.

Eighteen

'Christ, it's very empty here, isn't it?'

'Yeah, hello,' laughs Maud. 'What did you expect, sky-scrapers?'

Carrying our weekend bags and plastic bags of shopping, we're walking across the dunes towards our cottage.

Frank peers out over the sea and takes a deep breath. 'Wonderful, that sense of space.'

I follow his gaze. There are all kinds of things you could say about Ameland, but not that it's overpopulated. There's a father kicking a ball about with his son on the beach, and I can see a few people strolling on the horizon. That's it.

Maud points to a few cottages in the distance, up on a dune.

'Yes. That must be it.' Frank nods.

We walk further along the dune path.

'That's the one,' pants Frank. 'Number three.'

Now I understand why we were able to book a cottage two days before the weekend. The shutters of our rental cottage are hermetically sealed.

Frank sticks the key in the lock and opens the door. We walk straight into the sitting-room. There's an octagonal brown glass coffee-table, the kind you only see in TV documentaries about sink estates. There's a Joy-of-Painting-style picture on the wall.

'Hmm,' says Maud.

'OK. A change is as good as a rest,' mutters Frank.

We burst out laughing. The design police would come down hard on beach-house number three, if they saw it. I throw my weekend bag on the leatherette sofa.

This weekend is Frank's initiative. The Dinner Club on tour. Just Maud, him and me. No Dollies, no Natasha, no Ramon and no Rose. 'So that we can have a bit of peace and a nice chat.'

Carmen's mother is looking after Luna this weekend, at my house. When I told her after the third cup of coffee that Papa and Frank were really, really going away, she burst into tears. Yet again. At the moment I can't move an inch without her bursting into tears. That business with the tram left its mark.

On the boat, thank God, I get a text from Carmen's mother saying that peace has returned in Amsterdam. Luna is enjoying the seals at the zoo.

Maud's going to cook this weekend. We've got enough food here for an orphanage. Frank supplied wine and champagne, I brought the vodka and lime. At Frank's urgent request there are no drugs. 'Let's get away from the nose-candy for a while.'

■

We haven't talked so much for weeks. The last two Dinner Club Mondays were called off at my instigation.

As we stroll along the beach, Frank tells me how things are going at MIU. He's taken on a new junior account executive on probation, and if that works we'll do better this year than we did last. Volkswagen has a new marketing manager, and he's given us a contract that will keep three people busy for months. I feign interest, but realize I'm not exactly enthralled.

Maud says that last weekend she had a date with a guy from the gym and slept over at his place. She isn't about to repeat the experience.

I tell them I went to Antwerp with Rose for the weekend.

'How serious are things between the two of you?' asks Frank. I skim a stone across the sea.

'Not at all,' I reply. 'It's nice being with her, but I deliberately keep my distance when we've spent a weekend together like that.'

Frank wants to know how.

'Towards the end of the weekend I mention in passing I won't be seeing much of her during the week because I've got other appointments.'

'And then he shags a Dolly,' adds Maud with a laugh.

'Really?' Frank asks with surprise. 'But that can't be so great, one so soon after the other?'

Maud bends down to pick up a shell.

If only he knew that after every meeting of the Dinner Club she sleeps at mine.

■

Over dinner we play Carmen's CD. Frank says he's worried we're all living like nothing's happened. He says he's two days behind because he went home with that Dolly after the party.

'It didn't feel good. I felt guilty towards Carmen, as if I wasn't feeling any grief.'

Maud and I think he's talking nonsense. 'Carmen always thought you should be having more sex,' Maud says positively.

'You bet,' I reply. 'Even if you shagged a goat.'

'Well, a sheep's the second-best thing,' Frank says shyly.

We roll around on the table with laughter.

■

The CD's on track six. *'I want to spend my life with a girl like you,'* sing the Troggs. My eyes brim with tears. Maud and Frank weep along with me when I tell them about my last dance with Carmen.

We slowly get drunk.

At half past two Frank gets up and hugs us. 'Good wine, delicious food and fine friends. What more could you want from life?' We kiss each other goodnight.

'Goodnight, that was a great day, my friends,' he says with a yawn.

I say I'm going to stay up for a while and, when Frank isn't looking, pinch Maud on the arm.

Nineteen

'It's always nice to have a little something set aside.' I open my hand and show Maud a piece of silver paper.

She looks at it, and then at me. 'No – you can't be serious.'

'As long as it doesn't bother Frank, it doesn't matter, does it?'

Without waiting for her answer, I unfold the little package and spill the contents carefully onto the glass table. I take a banknote out of my bag and roll it into a tube.

After wiping my nose, I pass the roll to Maud. She's dubious for a moment. 'Oh, why not,' she says. 'Happy landing.'

■

Maud's eyes are spinning. One of her legs is thrown over the edge of the sofa and the other one's up in the air. I'm lying on top of her, thrusting hard against her body.

'You want it,' I whisper in her ear. My dick feels like it's on fire.

Maud squints. 'Take me,' she says in a hoarse voice, 'you can do anything you like with me . . .'

My eye falls on the bottle of champagne we opened a little while ago.

'Wait a sec.'

I pick up the bottle, put it to my mouth and take a good swig. Then I dive between her legs. I open her lips with my fingers, and carefully let the champagne pour over her vulva.

'Yessssss . . .' sighs Maud.

I lick her, and look up towards her torso. She's stuffed a corner of the sofa cushion into her mouth to mute her moans. She's moving more and more wildly, her breasts heaving up and down.

She comes with a shudder.

I kneel down and bring my dick back towards her drenched pussy. I look down and watch as I push it slowly between the lips. I pour the last of the champagne over her belly, her breasts and her open mouth. I throw the empty bottle into the corner of the room. Maud screams, throws her legs back to her shoulders and claws at my back with her fingernails. I growl and pound my dick harder and harder inside her.

And then Frank comes into the room in his underpants.

Twenty

Frank's eyes glide around the room. I see him looking at the empty champagne bottle. And then at Maud. At Maud's white knickers on the edge of the sofa. At my shoes. At the rolled-up ten-euro note. At the silver paper. And at the remains of the coke. Then he turns round, walks out of the sitting-room and slams the door.

Maud is the first to speak.

'Shit – oh, this is really shit. Come on, stand up!'

I stand up numbly and look around for my boxer shorts.

By now Maud is pulling her jeans on. She leaves her knickers where they are. She grabs my T-shirt and puts it on.

'I'll go and see Frank,' she says in a quavering voice.

Dazed, I sit on the sofa for a few minutes. I stare at the Joy-of-Painting painting. What a lot of trees.

Then I hear the door open.

'So, how is he?' I ask without looking.

No reply.

I turn my head towards the door and look right into Frank's red-rimmed eyes. He's holding his weekend bag. The zip is open.

'I'm going.'

'Oh?' I don't look at him. 'Well, you do what you must.'

Frank steps over my legs, opens the front door and disappears into the night.

I take the vodka bottle from the table and put it to my mouth.

I hear Maud sobbing in the next room.

Twenty-one

'How's Lan – erm – your daughter?' asks Natasha.

'She's well!'

'Oh. Good.'

'Yes. Very good.'

Natasha is sitting next to me playing with her bracelets. I flick through the in-flight magazine.

'And what's going on with Frank?'

'How d'you mean?'

'He's been so abrupt at work. You spent last weekend on Ameland, didn't you?'

'Yes.'

'Maud called in sick on Monday.'

'Really?'

'Yes. She came back yesterday. Frank didn't say a word to her all day. There's been a boring crowd at MIU since you've been away, but it's impossible to get through the day like this.'

I sigh.

'So?'

I hesitate. 'Frank's a bit fed up with the whole business.'

'The whole business?'

'Yes,' I snap. 'Us. He hates the fact that we're all doing coke. And that everybody's – ' I make the screwing gesture with my thumb between my fingers.

'Ridiculous. We just like each other.' Natasha turns towards the seat on the other side of her. 'Ramon, what do you think?'

Ramon turns off his Walkman.

'Don't you think it's been nice the way we've all been getting on lately?'

He shrugs and nods. And puts his headphones back on.

'Frank doesn't think so, Dan tells me. But what I think is,' Natasha adds, 'if you go to bed together, it only makes the friendship stronger.'

I stare out of the window and think of what Frank said.

'Something happened last weekend, didn't it?'

I realize my face is starting to turn red.

'Oohoo, look, Ramon, Dan's blushing.' Natasha nudges Ramon. 'Gather round!' cries Natasha. Two Dollies in front of us turn round. I start telling the story.

'And then, and then?' squeals the Dolly on the left.

'And then Frank took his weekend bag from the bedroom and cleared off.' I don't mention the fact that his eyes were red, or that Maud said in the morning that she wished she was dead.

Natasha and the Dollies shriek. Ramon grins.

'I don't think it's all that weird,' says Natasha. 'Coke makes you incredibly horny.' The Dollies nod.

'Frank has to understand that it's just a phase, Danny. In your situation you can't do what everybody wants you to do,' says Ramon. 'Women cry their misery away, men shag it away.'

Natasha agrees that it's just a phase. 'Frank's just jealous of you, you know.'

The light above our seats comes on and the stewardess announces that we have to fasten our seatbelts because the captain has announced the descent to Ibiza.

Twenty-two

Ramon walks nonchalantly through customs, through the sliding doors and into the safe entrance hall. I run sweating after him.

'You see? Not a problem,' he says with a grin.

'Sshhhttt!' I hiss.

He laughs and pinches my cheek. 'Welcome to Ibiza, Danny!'

Giggling, the Dollies join us, with beauty cases the size of cool-boxes.

'Oooh, and I've stuffed my bits full of coke and pills,' coos Natasha. She's jumping up and down so much that I'm worried the whole cargo is going to come clattering out. Has she brought it all the way from Amsterdam in her—? And won't it go off in there?

I see other relieved expressions among the passengers. If they'd turned our plane upside down, Ibiza would have been buried under a snowfall that would put Alaska to shame.*

Long live Schengen.

■

---

* Freely wrampled from *Life of Pi*, Yann Martel (2001).

My jaw drops as we park our mid-range hire-car outside the gate of our temporary accommodation in Ibiza. The place is even more beautiful than it looked on the Internet, a blind man could see that in a second. The house we're encamped in this week is white, big, with mountains in the background, a swimming pool in the foreground and in the distance a blue sea in which a person might spontaneously turn into a dolphin.

Ramon, who has been to Ibiza thousands of times, has arranged it all. He scores points today. The Dollies walk around oohing and aahing. The teak deckchairs are lined up smartly in a row beside the swimming pool, and there's a stainless-steel thing that looks like a spaceship, but which on closer inspection turns out to be a supersonic barbecue. The landlord has filled the Smeg fridge to the brim with complimentary bottles of cava and San Miguel. And to think that for the next few days a flock of topless Dollies is going to be gambolling around the place. I feel as if I'm in a Jackie Collins novel.

Even inside, the house is gigantic. It's practically Melrose Place. There's an endless number of bedrooms. I choose one on the second floor, reckoning that it'll be quieter there, and unpack my case.

We're staying here for a week, but with the number of shirts and T-shirts that I've crammed into my suitcase it looks more like I'm emigrating. I'm scared stiff of being overdressed or underdressed. According to Ramon, there's not much risk of that, there are no dress codes in Ibiza, he says. He walks around looking like a surfer. Opening times of clubs, when we have to go where, the right beaches and beach bars, he knows the lot. I wouldn't be surprised if he could predict the weather for the coming week, as well.

The sound of shrieking comes up from the swimming-pool terrace. I look out the window and see that the first Dolly has shed her clothes and dived into the pool wearing nothing but a tiny string bikini. Ramon, with his irritating washboard belly, grabs the second one by the waist ('No, no, don't!') and jumps in after the first Dolly with the screaming girl. On the terrace, a few steps higher up, I see Natasha bending over the CD player. She too has unpacked her impressive breasts, and is sticking a CD into the machine. I hear a cheerful synthesizer ditty and a voice singing a line that I think I know from Toto. Still swimming, the Dollies join in as if it was a folk song. '*If I hed unoddur chence tonaaait,*' they sing at the tops of their voices. When the drum machine comes in and settles into a heavy beat, Natasha sets the thing to permanent bother-the-neighbours volume and starts jumping. Her breasts fly around in a circle. It's a good thing I chose a room on the second floor, or they'd have whacked me in the face. Grinning, I hoist myself quickly into my trunks, put on a loose, short-sleeved shirt to avoid having to compete with Ramon, and come down the steps. The third Dolly is just bringing a tray of pieces of Manchego and *jamón* out of the kitchen. I take a slice, slap her playfully on the bum and kiss her on the cheek. She bites at me, her tongue sticking out, and says with a playful wink that this is going to be a really fun week.

Twenty-three

An hour later I'm pissed as a parrot.

I'm standing in the swimming pool waving my second bottle of cava, and I'm having more fun than Luna has with her little friends in an inflatable pool. I swim to the edge and rest my arms on it. The view is phenomenal. Dolly III is lying on a deckchair with her legs half open. She's busy rubbing coconut-scented oil over her breasts. My eyes are doing overtime, flitting back and forth from her glistening breasts to the point where the white string disappears into her crotch. I reckon there's quite a good chance that I might make the same journey myself later this week.

'Tatatatatáá̇á!!!' shrieks Natasha from the doorway, with a new tray in her hands. From my spot in the swimming pool I can't see what's on it, but it isn't hard to guess. The Dollies rush to the tray like children running after a football.

I look at my watch. Christ alive, it's two in the afternoon. I hesitate about whether to make a few paternal observations over the choice of menu at this time of day, but apart from me no one seems to be the slightest bit bothered. Ramon snorts the first line, and the Dollies meekly follow. I observe the spectacle with some surprise.

Natasha looks at me invitingly, from the other side of the pool.

'It's fun, darling!' she calls.

I laugh and shake my head. 'Maybe later.' I'd like to keep my consumption down a little this week.

I see Natasha whispering something in Ramon's ear. He looks over his shoulder at me as if I'm a referee insisting that the ball has to be five centimetres further back for a free kick. Oh, what do I care? Is it worth being a misery-guts in this idyllic place, just because it's too early for a social snort?

A quarter of an hour later I'm no longer a parrot, I'm an über-parrot. We're the Dutch team in 1974 and the Allies in 1944 at the same time.[*]

The house music from the CD-player booms out over the valley. I hear a song that I vaguely know from the Pilsvogel.

'Christ, what fantastic music,' I call across from a lounger, 'what is it?'

'Raven Maize!' shrieks Natasha above the music. 'Do you like it, babes?'

'Louder!' I roar. Natasha laughs and pushes the buttons till the sound starts distorting. Even though the nearest villa is so far away we're unlikely to disturb anyone, we really are trying our hardest. This is our island.

From behind my sunglasses I look out over my kingdom. Ibiza is at my flip-flopped feet. I look around at the wooded mountains. At the austere blue light. At the sea. At the far-off beach, full of losers who can't afford a house like this one.

Dolly II lies glistening on an air-bed in the pool. Her

---

[*]   Wrample from *Hyper*, Jacob van Duijn (2005).

sunglasses cover half of her face. She moves her head to the rhythm of the music. Her lips are pursed. Every now and again she licks her upper lip with the tip of her tongue, a delicious piece of blonde confectionery. She's number one on my wish-list for this week. On the other side of the pool, Ramon bends over another Dolly with his washboard stomach. Even in that posture I can't see a bit of flab, however hard I look. He blows over the Dolly's stomach with a straw. She giggles. Every now and again he strokes her left nipple with the straw, the rat. I stare enthralled at her tits. Jesus Christ, they're getting hard as well. My trunks are swelling with an almost painful erection. I tap it with my fingers, to the rhythm of the music. 'OK, Dan?' grins Dolly II from her air-bed.

'Horny,' I shout, trying to be heard above the music.

'I can see.'

I look at her. Oh, what the fuck!

'What time does the shagging start?' I shout, pull my trunks down a little, take my stiffy in my right hand and start waving it about as if it's a cocktail shaker.

Dolly II roars with laughter, and Ramon's Dolly also darts an amused look in my direction.

Washboard–cocktail shaker: 1–1.

I grin and feel good. What am I saying, I feel like God. I get up, pull off my trunks, take a run and, with a yell, plunge into the water right beside the terrace.

Always a laugh with Dan.

When I surface, no one's laughing. Everyone's looking at me with horror. 'Dan, what have you done!?' yells one of the Dollies.

'You almighty great twat!' roars Ramon, 'you've soaked it!'

92

I can't understand why they're making such a fuss about a few chair cushions, until I see Ramon furiously trying to salvage a pile of coke.

'Idiot,' snaps Natasha, 'you know that was several hundred euros' worth of charlie?'

In record time my popularity plummets to rock bottom. I stammer that I'll claim back the damage on my travel insurance.

Twenty-four

My mouth tastes a like rotten muskrat and, worse than that, there's an irritating sawing noise coming from very close by. I'm going to turn round. Ow! Gently, Danny, gently. I make a second attempt. Beside me there's a woman snoring. Oh, yes. Dolly II. On the bedside table I see a silver bowl with some remains of Partyman's Friend. My God, she looked so hot last night, when she sat on me like that. Better than now. Her half-open mouth is producing the most unerotic noises, and there are a few caked grains under her nose.

For a moment I consider stopping her snoring by stuffing my morning erection into her half-open mouth, but my thumping head protests. Dolly is still lying with her legs wide open. That looks pretty tasty. Pubic hair is clearly out of fashion at the moment. I get my camera from my suitcase, go and sit between her legs and take two photographs.

Then I pick up my phone to see if I've had any more messages.

Shit!

Frank.

> Don't need to see you again. But we've got
> to sort out what we're doing with MIU.

Pretty important.

I text back.

Make a bid.

I slowly get up, walk across the landing and open the door of the room next to mine. Occupied. Ramon with, by the looks of things, Natasha. The door of the next room is open. I slump down on the empty bed. Fuck, we did some drinking yesterday. Even after dinner at Bambuddha I was completely arseholed. If I hadn't snorted down industrial quantities of coke in the toilets, I'd have spent the whole night hallucinating. That would have been a sin. I've rarely felt as good as I did last night, there, up on the stairs, looking down on the crazy crowd at Space, while Fatboy Slim was Dj-ing. Fatboy Slim. Life doesn't get much more fun than that. How I ever made it to the age of thirty-seven without doing this island is a complete mystery to me. Ibiza should be a compulsory part of everyone's education.

Shame about my head, though. This takes the hangover into a new dimension.

In a bit I'll have a nice long shower.

Another six days to go.

Twenty-five

It was pretty disgusting, Dolly II tells me by the pool.

I've forgotten what and where I stuck what, and shrug. 'Yeah, I can't even remember when I came.'

'You didn't,' she replies cheerfully, her mouth full of cracker and hazelnut spread. 'You finally went to sleep with a limp dick, half on top of me.'

The plenary session on the terrace splutters with laughter. The contents of the recently opened packet of conviviality nearly blows over the table.

I'm glad that I get a text, so that I can stoop down for a moment and my red face isn't too conspicuous.

It's Anne.

> Luna and Lindsey built a very high tower
> out of Lego. A piece of MA: give her a call
> later on and ask her about it, because she
> was very proud.

Ouch!

Luna.

I haven't been in touch, I haven't thought of her for even a moment. She nodded when I asked her if she was looking forward to it, as we packed her little Winnie-the-Pooh suitcase together. Pyjamas, clothes, story-book, dummy and of course, Poppy. Poppy is the name of the cuddly Waldorf doll that Anne gave her.

While we were on the way to Maarssen, Luna nodded enthusiastically when I asked her if she was looking forward to her stay. I told her Papa would be back after a few sleeps, and that it would be really, really nice with Lindsey and, erm – Thomas and Anne's other children.

As I drove away and saw Luna sitting on Anne's arm, waving sadly at me, I felt like a traitor. And it didn't help much that Rose, when we were having coffee at De Gruter, said she didn't think it was all that clever of me to go away for another whole week without Luna, right after Ameland.

I look out over the valley and feel tears coming to my eyes. Without looking at the gang, I go inside to hide them.

I'm going to phone Luna. Now.

Anne answers. She tells me that Luna has just started her afternoon nap ('It's a quarter past one!'), that she slept well last night, got up very early this morning, at half past six, that she's been eating very well, particularly last night's pasta with melted cheese, which went down very nicely. Luna's a bit sniffly, because it's cold in Holland and I should really have given her a jumper, but all in all she thought she was doing well. Especially with Lindsey, those two play so nicely together. Anne tells me in great detail about the Lego tower.

Meanwhile I go back outside and take a slice of chorizo from a bowl. I pick up an open bottle of cava and fill up my glass. I gesture to Natasha, asking if she wants some, too. She nods.

'Ramon, is this glass yours or mine?' she asks Ramon,

who is sitting at the table next to her flicking through a magazine.

'Darling, do you think I give a stuff if I'm drinking out of your glass?' he replies without looking up. 'Last night I spent a quarter of an hour licking out your pussy.'

The Dollies squeal with laughter. Ramon looks up and gestures irritably at me to hang up. To save face I make a nodding motion and pretend to yawn.

Anne goes on chatting merrily.

'– although you can tell that she's an only child, she has trouble standing up for herself, particularly when everyone here is talking over everyone else at the dinner table.'

I answer sharply that it wasn't the plan for Luna not to have a brother or sister, but that something happened to Carmen. Ramon grins. He calls across that it might be funny if I told Anne all the things I got up to with Dolly II last night. I tell Anne I've got to go because we're going out and I'll phone Luna later on.

Twenty-six

Natasha warns me that coke and E aren't an ideal combination. I suspect she's just jealous.

'Bugger off and nag someone else,' I snap, 'you're not my fucking mother!'

We're in Amnesia, and I've just been given a pill by an absolutely gorgeous woman from London.

A moment later, when I'm screwing her in a toilet, the door suddenly flies open and I'm grabbed from behind by a gorilla with a blue suit and a tie, who drags me by the neck through the dancing crowd and throws me out. 'Fuck off, you fucking arsehole!' he shouts by way of farewell.

A little later I'm lying on my back on the gravel by the entrance. I indignantly crawl to my feet, yelling insults that I heard the great Dutch footballer Johan Cruyff in his heyday shouting at Spanish referees. Then I leg it, loudly announcing to the waiting people that I'm never setting foot in that stupid club ever again.

I receive pitying looks.

Once I'm round the corner I remember that I haven't got a mobile with me, so I can't even ring Ramon and the girls to tell them I've ended up in a rotten state. It isn't yet three o'clock, and Amnesia shuts at seven. There isn't much point waiting till they come out, so I hail a taxi.

■

I feel really sad in the big villa, knowing that the rest are freaking out on the dance-floor and will probably be away for hours.

My footsteps echo through the house. I look at my phone. No texts, no missed calls, no one who misses me. The sods! In the bathroom I look in the mirror and give a start when I see my reflection. I look white, my eyes are red. In the most luxurious villa they've plonked down on this mountainside I feel abandoned, while all the people who could cheer me up are in Amnesia, Amsterdam, Maarssen or wherever. I walk outside, go and stand next to the pool and launch a kick at the deckchairs. I open the fridge, grab a bottle of cava and hurl it over the fence of our villa. I hear it land with a dull thud somewhere in the woods. My eyes search for a heavy object to vent my anger on. Yes. There. A plant-pot with a palm. I hoist the heavy great thing in the air and swing it into the pool. The palm floats. I stare at it for a moment, and then slump down on to one of the teak deckchairs. I pick up my mobile and try to call Ramon. Then Natasha. No one answers. I tap in a text.

> **I'm at home. Thrown out of Amnesia. Feel abandoned. Please phone.**

I look at my address book, under R. Shall I? My heart thumps in my throat. The phone rings three times. Then I'm put through to her voicemail. Given the brush-off. 'Hello, this is Rose. I'm not here at the moment. If you leave a message, I'll call you back.'

I'm uncertain for a moment. When the beep sounds, I say I miss her and quickly hang up. It's half past four. It'll still be at least two or three hours before anyone comes home. That's if they don't go straight to Space, the after-party that Ramon was talking about yesterday. What now? I have less chance of getting off to sleep now than I have of playing in Ajax's first eleven. Is there any stuff in the house?

I walk into Ramon's room. I find a little envelope in a side pocket of his suitcase. I go into the bathroom and lay out a line on the edge of the basin.

The white stuff helps. Within a few minutes I'm more horny than lonely. I make a fierce attempt to bring myself to orgasm, but discover after ten minutes that it threatens to be an open-ended session. I go into the Dollies' bedrooms and snuffle around in their drawers. I'm particularly turned on by Dolly IV's blue string, which has a little pineapple on the back. In Dolly II's room I discover a little vibrator among her things. I also see a diary there, and can't help reading it for a moment. Go on. I read that I fucked her ruthlessly up her artist's entrance. I stare at the last sentence in the diary.

'It was like being raped.'

Twenty-seven

The phone rings.

Or an alarm clock goes off.

No, it's my mobile!

I jump up off the bed and run to my own room.

Where is the bloody thing? Oh. There.

Natasha.

'Daaarling!' she shrieks.

I look at my watch. Eight o'clock.

I here beach noises. 'Hi. Where are you all?'

'Ramon's lying buck naked in the sea, I'm here with a couple of really nice guys from Barcelona, there are two sweet girls from Limburg, and – let's see, oh, yes, we've found two people from The Hague and, oh, here comes Ramon . . .'

The phone is wrenched from her hand.

'Hi, you tosser!'

'Ramon. You OK?'

'Where've you been, you halfwit? What sort of bollocks is that, getting thrown out?'

'From what I hear, I wasn't much missed.'

'Stop whingeing, you prick. Grab a taxi and come to Playa d'en Bossa. We're going to Space in an hour.'

'Hmm.' The only thing that sounds worse than that is being alone for a few hours.

'Come on. Now! I'll save one of these Limburg chicks for you.'

'Will you wait?'

'Yes. But hurry up. And pick up a bit of fun from my room. There's a bag in the side packet of my suitcase.'

I'd already found it. There's still half a snort in it, which I've transferred to a piece of silver paper and then stuffed in my trouser pocket.

■

The atmosphere is stressed when we step into Space at half past nine in the morning. Ramon, Natasha, the Limburg chicks, the Dollies and their blokes from The Hague, our new friends from Barcelona, everyone walking around here has clearly swallowed or snorted a reserve dose of energy just before I showed up. Great, it means that for the time being there won't be any questions from Ramon about what happened to his own supplies.

InBedWithSpace is the name of this morning's party. I'd seen it on billboards this week, on the way from the airport to our castle, but I'd thought that the a.m. after the 9 was a joke.

I'm watching the crowd the way Dutch goalkeeper Jan Jongbloed watched the shot with which Gerd Müller brought the score to 1–2 in the '74 World Cup Final.

Natasha comes to my aid.

'Not feeling so great, darling?'

'Well . . .'

'Come here.'

She pushes me into one of the sitting areas on the edge of the dance-floor, rummages around in her handbag and inconspicuously holds her hand under my nose.

A quarter of an hour later I'm dancing.

■

Half past two. In the afternoon. I'm shagged out. I've been wandering around whingeing for half an hour, asking if anyone would like to come with me to one of the restaurants outside.

'Tash, aren't you hungry?'

'No, darling, we're carrying ooonnn!'

'Ramon, bite to eat?'

'Fuck off, you wanker, we're not there yet.'

'Alfredo, erm – *mangiare?*'

'*Que?*'

'Food? Hungry? Outside? Oh – fuck it!'

Three-quarters of an hour later I finally get them to come along.

The man behind the desk at the restaurant frowns when he sees us coming in screeching and laughing.

'Oi, tosser,' Ramon roars from a distance, 'do me one of them Italian cowpats.'

'Pizza!' shrieks Natasha from one of the tables. She bangs her cutlery on the table. The Dollies and the girls from Limburg follow her example. I order a hamburger.

By the time it shows up, the whole brigade's back outside again. I look around and see them walking a little further along the street. It's a weird sight, a group of party-goers in full get-up, in broad daylight, completely trolleyed. The Limburg girls are walking on blue shoes with heels like pile-dwellings, the Dollies are wearing fluorescent wigs, one of the guys from The Hague – a ludicrously handsome boy with long blond hair – is wearing a cowboy hat, and Ramon's wearing Elton-John-format sunglasses.

Still eating, we walk towards the beach.

'Shall we go to Bora Bora for a bit?' calls a Dolly with her mouth full of pizza.

'Let's have a look here, first,' calls Ramon.

A great crowd is standing by one of the outdoor cafes with big TV screens constantly showing Premier League matches. The people are standing in the street. As we get closer I hear someone scream. I see a boy staring open-mouthed at the screen, and a girl has both hands over her mouth.

'Come on, this looks like fun!' calls one of the Limburg girls.

'Yoohoo, we're keepin' on!' screeches Tash.

A few people look around, irritated, and gesture to us to be quiet.

'Hey, mind your own business,' shouts the guy from The Hague with the hat.

'Shut your mouth, arsehole!' someone shouts back.

I take a few steps to the side and see that everyone's staring perplexedly at the screen. Have I forgotten an important Champions League match? No, it's Tuesday afternoon.

'A live video game,' I hear Ramon yelling. He's climbed on to a chair.

There's more screaming. *There goes another one!* I hear someone yell.

'*FUCK! NO!!!*' wails a boy somewhere towards the front.

'Hey, you've got to see this, sweetie!' says the tall guy

from The Hague to the Dolly next to me. 'They're flattening that skyscraper! Hell, what a fantastic sight!'

He lifts the Dolly up so that she can see over people's heads. 'You'll get a repeat in a second. This is way cool!'

A man with a bare beer-belly covered with tattoos turns round. His wife is pressed tightly to him. She's crying. The man's eyes spit fire. 'Fuck off, you, right now!' he yells at the guy from The Hague.

I climb onto a car. When I'm on top, I can see a skyscraper collapsing with a lot of smoke. CNN. People running away in panic, the camera going in all directions, hang on – that looks like New York. A little frame appears in the corner of the screen. It *is* New York, damn it! It's the World Trade Center. It's the fucking WTC! In the frame, plumes of smoke rise from one of the two towers. A dot with a circle drawn round it is flying towards the second tower. The picture is shown in slow motion. The people in the café start screaming again. A text appears at the bottom of the picture.

Fourth plane said to have crashed into the Pentagon ***
US under attack *** One of Twin Towers has collapsed ***
President Bush evacuated to a secure location.

I look beside me. Ramon is whooping, he's taken off his shirt and he's waving it round his head. He looks at me with a grin and sticks his thumb in the air. I look at the rest of the group. Natasha has gone to sit on the kerb and is eating her pizza. She's having a chat with one of the girls from Limburg. The guy from The Hague has stuck his hand down the back of one of the Dollies' trousers. She laughs and pulls his hand away. I look at the screen again. New York. World Trade Center. Pentagon. The guy from Barcelona asks if I want some more, and shows me a little bag of powder in his hand. Another Dolly says loudly that she's getting bored here with the TV and she wants to move on.

It's as if all the sound has been turned off. I see the second tower collapsing.

All of a sudden I think of Luna. Oh my God! Luna. *I'll carry on, however difficult it might sometimes be. And I'll take good care of your daughter.* This is turning into war. This is war. Tomorrow Iraq will be flattened. Or Moscow. Or what do I know. *And I'll take good care of your daughter.* I look at my friends and see they're still laughing. I've got to get away. I've got to get the fuck away from here. I jump down off the car. *And I'll take good care of your daughter.*

A taxi drives past. I run after it till it stops.

For the whole journey I can only think of one thing. *And I'll take good care of your daughter.* I grab my phone and, with trembling fingers, dial Anne and Thomas's number.

'Dan?!' weeps Anne. 'Have you seen? What on earth's happening?'

I mumble that it's a terrible business. She starts crying even harder.

And for the first time since I've known her, she thinks the same thing as me.

'Dan, how can we make sure our children are all right?'

Half an hour later I've changed my clothes and I'm packing my case. Even before the others get home, I'm in the taxi on the way to the airport.

> Ramon, I've left. I'm going to try to catch
> a flight tonight. I'm going to take care of
> my daughter.

Twenty-eight

'What were you thinking about when you phoned me this week? It was the middle of the night. Did you expect me to comfort you? Even on voicemail I could hear that you were completely out of it.'

'Yes, erm . . .'

'It's not good, Dan.'

'I really don't know any more, Rose. I'm at war, the whole world's at war . . .'

'Maybe you've got to do what you did after that car accident, when Carmen was still alive,' says Rose coolly.

'Do you think so?'

'You won't listen to me. Or Frank, so I gather.'

Twenty-nine

'So. It's been a long time.'

Nora shakes hands and looks at me with eyes that seem to pierce their way to the back of my brain.

> ► **Nora.** Spiritual therapist. Dan was informed of her existence by Rose, after his car accident/sex-and-drugs bacchanal/row with Carmen. Predicted that Carmen would soon die. Carmen's deathbed began that day, and Carmen & Dan finally had a happy ending. Quote: 'Now you have the chance to give back to your wife what you had from her for all those years.'

'Yes,' I answer, embarrassed. 'I thought it was time to come back.'

She smiles. 'Come right in. You know the way. Would you like some tea?'

'I'd love some.'

She lays her hand on my shoulder. 'I'm glad you're here, Dan.'

'Thanks. Me too, I think.' It's an unfamiliar luxury, visiting a woman you have no chance of ending up in bed with. Nora is even less attractive than Anne. A comforting thought.

'What made you think of honouring me with a visit again?' she calls from the kitchen.

'Rose. Before I forget: she told me to say hello.'

'That's nice,' Nora calls back. 'How is she?'

'Oh –' Not much has changed in Nora's consulting room. That painting with the waterfall and the purplish light is the only new addition to the collection I can see. There's music playing. I pick up a CD case. A black man with a huge flute. What do you call those things? A whistle with a growth spurt, about five feet long.

'No doubt she hoped you would become her boyfriend after Carmen's death?' her voice echoes from the kitchen.

It always takes a long time, with these spiritual types.

'Yes. She's really sweet, but I can't think about having a girlfriend. All that possessive stuff gives me boils.'

Nora grins. 'Well, maybe she loves you too much to be able to let you go.'

'Then she'll have to learn.'

'I agree with you there.'

'Good.'

'Do you like the nice music?' asks Nora, coming in with a teapot, two cups and a plate of biscuits.

I quickly put the CD case down.

'Ehm – bit funny, isn't it?' I reply.

'It's Aboriginal,' she laughs.

'Ah. I couldn't place it exactly.'

She laughs and pours the tea. 'You can tell me if you don't like it, you know.'

'They play a different kind of music in Ibiza.'

She laughs again. 'I can believe that.' She goes and sits down. 'Was it hard to get a flight back? I'm sure everyone wanted to get home as quickly as possible.'

Last night, in the first train from Düsseldorf to Amsterdam, I received a text from Natasha. Paul Oakenfold in Pacha was just *da bomb*, Natasha wrote, with three exclamation marks and a keen sense of current affairs.

'It was hard to come back.'

'Perhaps. But you're happy to be back with your little girl.'

I nod. Yesterday, when I went to pick up Luna in Maarssen, she was in bed for her afternoon nap. I was immediately overwhelmed when I saw her. She was sound asleep, unaware of what the human race was doing to itself.

'Where does it go from here, Nora?'

'You or the world?' she smiles.

'Let's start with me,' I grin. 'That sounds quicker.'

She shakes her head. 'Nothing happens quickly, Dan. When you understand that, you'll have reached the end.'

She looks at me for a long time. I don't dare look back.

'Shall we talk about sex?' she asks all of a sudden.

Not her, too? I knew that SHAGGING has been written on my forehead over the past few months, but if even a spiritual counsellor thinks she … It doesn't bear thinking about. To save face, I quickly take a sip of my tea.

'Did you know that an enormous exchange of energy takes place during sex?'

'If it's good, yes,' I mumble. Forget it, you old witch.

'But things aren't good at the moment. You're being sucked dry. From all sides.'

I feel myself starting to blush.

'Nice bit of wordplay for an old person, don't you think?' she says mischievously. 'I think you've had enough of yourself for a while. Grieving takes energy. Your daughter needs energy. But sex costs you mountains of energy, too. The more partners you have, the more energy leaks away. And you're already starting to see it differently, too: you aren't getting anything back in return.'

OK, you can just stop right there. I'd probably say the same thing if I wasn't getting any.

'I could be wrong, I suppose. Maybe you feel more energetic when you've just been to bed with someone?'

'Hmm.'

'And drugs?'

'What about drugs?'

'Have you been doing a lot of drugs lately?'

'Well, you know, now and again. Just to be sociable.'

She looks at me.

I feel myself blushing again. 'I'm not in good shape, Nora.'

'Your wife is dead, Dan,' Nora says gently, 'you won't get her back with sex and drugs. Honestly.'

My eyes start filling.

'You know what's troubling you, Dan?'

I shake my head.

'Grief avoidance.'

'Grief avoidance?'

'How long has Carmen been dead now?'

'Three months, twenty-nine days and seventeen hours.'

'And when are you going to start grieving?'

Oh, here we go. 'Come on, Nora – am I supposed to shut down and act like I can't enjoy life now Carmen's not there any more? Jeez, I wrote Carpe Diem in great big letters on the wall! Do you really think Carmen wants me to walk around with an imaginary black armband?'

Nora looks at me, unmoved.

'You can't go on denying your emotions, Dan. You can

keep trying to run away, but you can't run away from yourself finally.'

'What, then?'

'Well, what do you really want?'

'Peace.'

'What's keeping you from it?'

'Everything. Drink. All those women. Going out. Drugs. Amsterdam. At the bottom of my heart I'd just like to go away, as far as possible, to – I dunno, Thailand, Australia.'

'So do it.'

'Oh, you can't just . . .'

'Why not?'

'Why not? Luna, my work, my friends.'

'You can take Luna with you.'

'Luna and me? Are you kidding?'

'She'd think it was fantastic, travelling with her father.'

'But isn't that running away, too? Dan can't cope in Amsterdam, so he just leaves.'

'And all these women aren't a form of escape?'

'. . .'

'There's only one person who can help you.'

'Who's that?'

'Luna.'

'Luna?'

'Luna.'

'But I spend lots of time with Luna,' I reply, horrified. 'We do loads of things together. We went to toddlers' ballet together and – hey, are you saying I'm a bad father or something?'

'No. I said *she* can help *you*.'

'Come on, Luna's three years old . . .'

'I know. But she gives you something all those women can't give you.'

'Like what? How can I expect my own daughter to help *me* when she's just lost her mother?'

'Luna can teach you how wonderful it is to love someone again. You remember how profound it felt to look after Carmen during her final weeks?'

I nod.

'Luna can give you that feeling again. By looking after her you'll rediscover the power of love. It's as simple as that.'

'Do I really have to go to the other side of the world to do that? Can't I find peace in a remote bit of Holland like the Veluwe forest? And we'd be far safer, too. I bet there isn't a single terrorist who knows where the Veluwe is.'

Nora laughs. 'Didn't Carmen go to Australia?'

'Carmen? Umm – yeah. The year before she met me. She travelled all across Australia, all by herself. Why?'

She picks up the CD case with the didgeridoo. 'Now I understand why I suddenly needed to put on this CD.' She hands me the CD case. 'Here. It's for you.'

'What do you mean by that? Is there something you know about Carmen that I don't?'

'Just take it with you.'

I stare at the case. Australia. Sounds good. A place for a fair-weather adventurer with a child in tow. Nice weather, normal food, normal people, normal toilets.

'Yeah, it sounds appealing, I must say,' I mumble.

'I think you'll find something in Australia.'

'Hmm. One of those big flutes on the CD case? Or a bushman to bring back as an au pair? Or The Woman Who's Going to Change My Life?'

She smiles and says nothing.

'And what about my work? I'm just back from Ibiza. I haven't done anything for three months. I can't leave Frank in the lurch again.'

Hmm. I suppose that problem resolved itself on Ameland.

'Sometimes you've got to dare to jump, Dan. Come on, it's time.'

She gets to her feet, pushes back her chair and takes the CD out of the CD-player. 'Here. Don't forget this.'

She opens the door of her consulting room and walks out into the hall ahead of me. 'Strength, Dan,' she says, offers me her hand and opens the door. 'Take care of your daughter. It'll sort itself out. Love is close by.'

■

In the car I look at the CD case. Behind the Aborigine I see an immense void. A whole continent of nothing. Clever boy who finds something there. And that's where I've got to go – with Luna. *I'll take good care of your daughter*. But day in, day out alone with Luna . . .

I sigh and put the CD of didgeridoo music into the player. Bloody hell!

Your taste in music doesn't get any better when you're dead.

Thirty

'Hi, Anne.'

'Hi, Danny.'

'Hi! How's Luna?'

'Fine!'

'She had a lot of fun here, didn't she?'

'Yes, she still talks about the food . . .'

'Well, if you ever want some time off again, just bring her over, we love having her here.'

'Now – to be honest – that's not what I'm ringing about, because, well actually, that won't be happening for a while . . .'

'Because of the terrorism? Yeah, I can imagine you don't really want to go away again for a while. I was just saying to Thomas: you won't see me in a plane for a while.'

'We're going to Australia.'

'I'm sorry?'

'We're going to Australia. First a week in Thailand, and then we're going to travel on to Australia.'

'Who's we?'

'Luna and me.'

'Both of you? You and Luna?'

'Yes.'

Silence.

'How did you come up with that?'

'I think I need to get away for a while.'

'With Luna? I'm not sure that's such a good plan, you know. Can we talk about it?'

'Anne?'

'Yes?'

'I booked it this afternoon. We're going in a week.'

Thirty-one

From: Frank@strategicandcreativemarketingagencymiu.nl
Sent: 16 September 2001
To: Danvandiepen@hotmail.com

Hi,

I've heard you're off to Australia. Your first wise decision in months. I hope you'll find yourself again.

Good luck,

Frank

PS: Whatever you do, make sure you take good care of Luna, for God's sake.

Thirty-two

Now I've booked it, I can't wait. I tell anyone willing to listen that Luna and I are going travelling. We fly in four days. First we're going to spend a week in Thailand to break the journey a bit for Luna, and then we're travelling on to Australia for an unspecified period of time. From Bangkok we fly to Cairns, in Queensland, north-eastern Australia. There we'll pick up our camper and drive all the way along the coast to the south.

But first I want to spend a few nights in Port Douglas, north of Cairns. Carm went to Port Douglas, I discovered in her photograph album. She looks fantastic and the backdrops are no less impressive – lots of blue sea, palm trees and beach, a little white church by the shore and photographs of a group of divers in the sea. All in Port Douglas, it says in the album. There are pictures of Sydney, the Great Ocean Road, and of Byron Bay, a place I've never heard of, but which is, according to the caption she's scribbled under the photograph, *Australia's No. 1 love-and-peace spot*.

When I'm looking through the kitchen cupboard for a Stanley knife to take out a few photographs, the bell rings.

Anne is standing on the doorstep. She stammers that she might have reacted a little quickly on the phone.

'I'd never do it myself, going on such a long journey with

my kids, but Carmen would definitely have thought it was a fantastic idea.'

I give her a hug. 'Come in, I'm just making some coffee.'

Luna shouts with joy when she sees Anne, and immediately jumps into her lap.

'I've brought you a present, sweetie,' says Anne, 'for when you're travelling with Papa.'

She gives Luna a little package. It contains a brightly coloured Walkman, with big buttons all over it. Anne takes a cassette out of her pocket, pops it in the Walkman and puts the headphones on Luna. I listen along, my head pressed against Luna's.

'Once upon a time there was a little girl. Everyone loved her, but her grandmother loved her best of all. Grandmother had made her a red bonnet of red velvet...'

'That's Grandma!' cries Luna with surprise.

I'm touched when I hear what Anne's been up to. She's gone to see everyone, armed with one of Lindsey's books of fairy tales, and had all our friends read one. Thomas is there, with 'The Pied Piper of Hamelin'. She herself has read 'Sleeping Beauty'. She even got Ramon to join in. His choice was 'The Wolf and the Seven Kids'. Before she came here, she called in at MIU with a cassette recorder. Maud did 'The Little Match Girl', and Tasha, just back from Ibiza, provided a giggling version of 'Snow White'. I gulp when I hear that even Frank is on there, reading 'Pinocchio'.

I reach out my hand across the table and stroke her arm. We look at each other in silence for a moment.

'I've got something else,' whispers Anne, while Luna listens open-mouthed to 'Little Red Riding Hood' as told by Carmen's mother.

'Just put this in your luggage where Luna won't see it.'

She takes an anthroposophical doll, the same as the one she gave Luna before, and passes it to me under the table. 'I know it's her favourite toy now. Just a bit of MA: a reserve doll is always a good idea. You really don't want to know what happens when a kid loses its cuddly toy.'

■

When Anne's left, I carefully prise out a couple of photographs with the Stanley knife and put them in my luggage. It's a nice idea, going with Luna to see the same places Carmen saw the year before we met.

Like she's still with us a little.

Thirty-three

Rose brought me a CD, *Play* by Moby, and a travelling set of Sesame Street Memory Game for Luna. Luna tells Rose about Anne's fairy-tale cassette. Tears well up in Rose's eyes. I gently mention that Anne left the book of fairy tales here 'in case other people come who know Luna'. Rose says she'd like to do her own reading session live, and asks if she can put Luna to bed tonight.

When she comes down, she tells me it was 'Hansel and Gretel'.

It promises to be an emotional evening. Her advice to go back and see Nora has indirectly ushered in the end of the duo 'Dan & Rose', inasmuch as such a unit ever officially existed. My departure from Amsterdam means it's over between us, once and for all.

After dinner we end up on the sofa. I put on the Moby CD. Rose lays her head in my lap.

'Will you be careful, with all these terrorist attacks?' she asks, her eyes closed.

I reply softly that I'll take great care, and stroke her hair. We sit in silence.

Moby sings 'Why Does My Heart Feel So Bad'. I see a tear trickling down her cheek.

Then she opens her eyes. 'I want to go to bed with you one more time,' she whispers.

Thirty-four

My bedroom window is half open. The curtains flutter in the wind.

I'm telling Rose about all the places I want to see in Australia and Thailand. I know it hurts her to hear my plans, but it's the only thing I can think of to keep this evening from ending too sadly.

Whenever things got difficult over the past six months, I escaped to Rose. When I couldn't bear the situation with Carmen any more, or after the car accident just before Carmen's death, or in the first few weeks after Carmen's death, after the E, the WTC and the coke misery on Ibiza, Rose has always been my emotional refuge.

But it's just too easy always to go back to her, to her safety and warmth. Now we're lying here naked in each other's arms, I know this is what I'll miss most of all.

'You'll be there in just a couple of days,' says Rose, interrupting my thoughts, as she runs her fingers through the hair on my chest. There's a tremble in her voice.

'Yeah . . .' I say softly.

Rose starts crying quietly.

I'd love to comfort her, tell her I'll be back in a few months, but I know things can never be the same between us. Rose and Dan without sex is impossible. We found that out while Carmen was still alive. Just cuddling? No, it would be a friendship doomed to failure. We can't keep our hands off each other. When I kiss her, I automatically feel her tongue darting into my mouth. When I hold her tight, my hands move of their own accord to her arse, her hips and the swell of her breasts. We could never have a platonic relationship.

I mustn't let myself dwell on the fact this is the last time I will ever feel her warmth.

I wish we'd gone on holiday one last time, for a week or even just a few days. As a goodbye. If I'd known what I know now, I'd have done that instead of going to Ibiza with those fuckwits.

All of a sudden I have a great idea.

Why don't I book that luxury resort in Koh Samui, that place that belongs to Frank's mate, the one he was talking about? They're bound to have a baby-sitting service. Jeez, from bingeing on drink, drugs and chicks in Amsterdam to a relaxed week in Koh Samui – and then the deep end. This way I can gradually get used to being with Luna day and night.

So the words just slip out of my mouth.

'Come with us to Thailand for the first week. A swansong.'

Rose lifts her head and stares at me like she's just seen a hippo knitting.

'OK!'

OK? Brilliant! Isn't Thailand just a pit-stop on the way? Doesn't the real work – no idea what that is, but that's how it feels – start in Australia?

A week, just the three of us, followed by a few months'

travel. A beautiful end to all we've meant to each other. What difference could it possibly make?

'Why not?'

'You really mean that?'

I must look really resolute, because her eyes start to twinkle. I lie that I'd thought of it earlier, and say we'll have to take a quick look tomorrow and see if there are any flights.

'Tomorrow?' she shrieks. 'But you're leaving the day after tomorrow. I'm going to look now!' She hugs me, jumps out of bed and puts on my dressing-gown.

'Is there a password on your pc?'

'Erm – yes . . .'

'And it's . . .'

'Carmie.'

■

As she walks downstairs I start fretting. Is this such a good idea? How am I going to explain it to everyone? I contemplate the ceiling.

■

'They're virtually all full,' I hear her calling in a disappointed voice.

A small wave of relief washes over me. It's a ludicrous, impulsive idea. But sometimes you have to bite the bullet. Stay of execution. It would only have ended in tears. Phew!

A quarter of an hour later Rose runs into the bedroom with a stack of printed A4 pages. She bounces over to the bed.

'I've found a flight to Bangkok,' she says, beaming, 'a day later than yours.'

'Oh. Great.'

She looks at me questioningly. 'Are you absolutely and totally sure? Because if you are, I'm going in to ask for time off from work . . .'

I hesitate for a moment. I look at her happy, expectant face. Her cheeks are pink with excitement.

'I'm sure,' I lie.

Rose kisses me, snatches her wallet from her jacket pocket, whips out her credit card and dashes back downstairs.

'Otherwise I'll lose that seat.'

I stare at the ceiling once more.

So, change of plans.

Rose is coming, too.

Thirty-five

Rose doesn't waste any time. Within an hour she's found the resort on Google. And booked it. It's called Kulay Pan, and we've got a suite by the sea, with a nursery. At a rate that could have bought me another two months in Australia.

There's hardly anything left for me to do. Rose concocts a list of things to take. There's a lengthy discussion about malaria injections. There are loads of phone calls, texts and emails with tips, plans and questions about everything *we* have to take with us.

We? I think, we? Luna and I are travelling for several months. You're coming along for a week.

To my relief, Luna is OK with it. She likes having Rose around.

But there's one major problem.

No one knows about it.

When Anne rang me this morning to give me some extra bits of MA, I didn't mention that Luna and I would be accompanied by a woman for the first week. And I didn't dare tell Maud, when she sent me a text this morning asking if there was anything else she should buy Luna for the holiday.

I'm more worried about Rose coming along on this trip

than I ever was about being seen with her when Carmen was still alive.

How in God's name can I explain I'm taking Rose with me? Carmen's mother hasn't got a clue about 'Dan & Rose'. And phoning Anne now to tell her I've taken her advice and decided to bring a girlfriend along doesn't seem such a good idea, either.

So I don't, and I ask Rose to do the same thing. 'It's all a bit sensitive, you understand, because of Carmen and everything.'

The only one who cottons on is Tasha. After I've said goodbye to everyone at MIU – one day when Frank's away visiting a client – I cycle back with her along the Stadionweg.

'You know what you're going to miss, don't you?' she asks.

'What?'

'Fucques les Balles, you *know*, the big gay party! The day after Christmas.'

I burst out laughing.

'Tasha, that's exactly the kind of thing I'm trying to get away from.'

'Oh. But you *are* looking forward to being alone with your daughter?'

'Of course I'm looking forward to it.'

'Why don't you take Rose along?' she says enthusiastically, visibly proud of her own brainwave.

I turn fiery red in a split second. I stubbornly look straight ahead.

Natasha gives me a sideways look and explodes. 'Woo-hoo, Dan! She is going with you, isn't she? Rose is going with the two of you, hahaha . . .'

'Just to Thailand,' I reply, embarrassed. 'One week.'

'Heeheehee – Danny, oh Danny – But, darling, it's sooo sweet!'

'Tash, please don't tell anyone.'

'My lips are sealed,' she sings, turns the key in an imaginary lock on her lips and throws it theatrically over her shoulder.

We go on cycling in silence.

'Know what I think, Dan?' she says suddenly as we're saying goodbye on the corner of Stadionweg and Minervalaan.

I shrug.

'I think that, after Thailand, Rose will go with you to Australia.'

Part Two

Dan & Luna
and Rose

Oh, how I love you, I think at the station
With the whole world all around us
And a voice says: will all passengers
For KL204 go to the departure lounge
Then you go through passport control
You look around and wave at me
I smile, but something dies in me
Because I know that it's really over too

Peter Koelewijn, from 'KL204 (Als ik God was),'
(*Het Beste in Mij is Niet Goed Genoeg Voor Jou*, 1978)

One

Luna can't stop staring. She's particularly interested in the tuk-tuks and the orange-robed monks. And Luna attracts plenty of attention herself. Every Thai waitress, every woman at a souvenir stand wants to touch her. *'Woohoo you pletty gul, hello!'* The greatest difference between Amsterdam and here is that it's Luna, not me, who's getting pestered by women. Blondes have more fun.

'Have you been here before, Pap?'

'Yes. Once.'

'With Mama?'

'Without Mama.'

Christ, what a drama that was, when Carmen freaked because I wanted to go on holiday solo. Rightly of course. Allowing Dan to go to Thailand for three weeks was really putting the cat among the pigeons.

'Why?'

'Why what?'

'Why without Mama?'

'Because I, erm – wanted to go on holiday by myself for once. You want to play without me sometimes, don't you?'

'No.'

'But you liked it when the lady in the restaurant took you to see the fishies, didn't you?'

'No.'

I look at her in surprise. 'Why not?'

'I want to be with you.'

And there was I thinking she enjoyed all the attention.

I just thought it was really sweet of the Thai girl to take Luna to show her the big fish in the aquarium at the back of the restaurant. It meant I could eat in peace for a moment.

'She cly,' laughed the girl when she brought Luna back. I thought Luna was crying because she was scared of the doggy-faced fish.

Luckily Rose is coming tomorrow. Otherwise I won't be able to take a crap on my own.

Two

We're a proper happy family.

All three of us go into the sea, all three of us go out to dinner, and all three of us go to a 'real authentic traditional Thai dance performance'. It's fantastic here.

Kulay Pan is heaven, and you don't even have to die to get there.[*] Every evening after one of us has read to Luna from the Dutch children's classic *Jip en Janneke*, Rose and I sit on our loungers on the terrace in front of our apartment, staring at the sea, clutching glasses of wine.

I'm enjoying the rest. Rose actually wants to see a bit of the island, but I insist that, apart from her body, there's nothing to look at here on Koh Samui. She mutters demurely a little for form's sake, but in reality she's absolutely delighted. She says it's the first time in six months I haven't been agitated.

And we don't have to worry about Luna, either. She's been full of beans since Rose arrived. She spends all day toiling with buckets and spades on the beach, which is practically outside our front door.

---

[*]   Wrample from *The Shadow of the Wind*, Carlos Ruiz Zafón (2004).

The sex is fantastic. It's probably because we know this is our last chance, or because we're ridiculously horny. Anyway we can hardly lay off each other all day. Sometimes I count the minutes till Luna's bedtime. We're so crazed with lust we can't think of enough things to do in bed. Rose is wilder than ever before. She wants to be blindfolded, she wants to be tied to the bars of the bed, she wants everything.

I don't let her down, either. I take pictures of her tits, her pussy, her giving me a blowjob, her on her knees, looking randily over her shoulder as I fuck her. It occurs to me that of all the women since Carmen, there isn't one with whom sex is as addictively delicious as it is with Rose. Rose and Dan is total fucking, *coitus mechanicus*, contours that fit together like a well-oiled machine. Nothing in the world smells as wonderful as her pussy when we've just had sex. What divine chemistry. The scent of Rose and Dan is manna to the nostrils.

And then the anatomy. Every nook, every fold inside her beats with every vein, every curve and engorgement of my stiff prick. It's like she was specially cast for me.

If I couldn't even come with the last of the Dollies, with Rose I've come prematurely more often than I have since my sixteenth birthday. It makes us both laugh as we lie there, side by side in each other's arms.

'We fit too well together,' I say with a laugh.

'Yeah, and that's why you're going to Australia next week,' Rose replies, suddenly sarcastic.

Three

'Shit!'

I'm checking my emails in the hotel lobby.

Maud. Things aren't going well at MIU. Frank only talks to her when he absolutely has to. They haven't looked each other in the eye once. And do I have Rose's phone number?; she wants to have lunch with her some time this week. She needs a chat, and thinks Rose might do, too, now that I'm in Thailand and Rose is still in autumnal Amsterdam.

Natasha emails to say she put her foot in it when Maud mentioned she'd tried phoning and emailing Rose a few times, but hadn't heard anything back. Maud is well pissed off, according to Tash. Thank Christ Maud isn't on speaking terms with Frank at the moment.

But the next email is from Frank. 'What are you up to, Dan?' is the only thing he writes.

I shut my Hotmail page and leave the lobby in a foul mood.

'Something up?' Rose asks anxiously when I get back to the beach with a face that looks as if I've just been sucking lemons.

'Nothing, except half of Amsterdam knows you're here.'

Four

My sense of self-worth, which I've been gradually restoring since my plucky decision to go away with Luna, has vanished at a stroke. The magic of the journey has gone. We're not a happy family and we never will be.

And I'm taking my frustration out on Rose.

The affectionate words of the first few days are fewer, replaced by abruptness. I decide where we're eating, with no consultation. I ask her to clean up her mess because it's turning into a massive great tip in here. I say I'm exhausted and don't feel like sex, and Luna will wake up early again tomorrow morning. And I make it clear that I, and no one else, decides when Luna gets her dummy and Poppy, and whether or not she has to leave a nice clean plate, and what time she has to go to bed. When Rose looks like she's about to help Luna, I give her a look that's pretty conclusive.

What's even more awkward is that, for the first time since I've known her, she doesn't know what to do with my moods. I can't just cry any more if she's around. As soon as something moves me, I change the subject, I go 'and get us a couple of drinks', or I 'really need a crap', and disappear to the toilet like a twerp.

Rose sees through me every time.

'Something up?'

'No, why?'

'Just thought . . .'

'Nothing's wrong.'

'Sure?'

'I said nothing is wrong.'

But everything's wrong, and Rose knows it. Luna just has to fart and I get a lump in my throat. Or she copies a Thai dancing girl with exaggerated movements, or takes my credit card to the waitress in a full restaurant and shyly asks, in English, '*Ken wie pei?*' or sits playing with her spoons, concentrating hard with the tip of her tongue darting out of her lips: definite tear-jerkers, every one.

Again and again we follow the same pattern:

1. I break off the conversation I'm having with Rose.
2. I look at Luna.
3. I stare at Luna.
4. The rest of the world ceases to exist.
5. I get choked, and start welling up.
6. Rose sees it and she gets choked, too, seeing me choked.
7. Rose tries to catch my eye.
8. I ignore Rose and cuddle Luna.
9. I smother Luna.
10. I whisper in her ear that I love her.

Then Rose starts feeling edgy, because half the terrace is watching this cuddly dad and a mum who looks a bit superfluous to requirements, like a reserve player warming up before the eyes of a full stadium, desperately trying to make eye contact with the coach to hear if she can finally come onto the pitch.

She can't.

In fact, at this rate, she's going to being relegated to the second eleven, a long way from the first, which is about to set off for the World Cup final in Australia.

Am I pushing her away because she said yes so gratefully when I asked, in a moment of weakness, if she wanted to come to Thailand? Am I pissed off with her for coming at all?

Whatever: it's doing nothing for the mood of the squad. Rose is about to be thrown out of the team, and I'm making less and less of an effort to keep up appearances. She may be feeling what I'm feeling: there aren't three of us on holiday, she's just here visiting 'Papa & Luna'.

My conduct has its effect. Rose grows more and more morose, and I therefore look forward, more and more, to my travels with Luna in Australia. I flamboyantly pick up the *Lonely Planet* guide to Queensland, where we're going first, and mark it up with lots of big arrows and circles.

The *Lonely Planet* guide to Thailand remains unmarked and unsullied.

Five

It's our last day on the island. To cheer things up a bit I've suggested a visit to the Monkey Farm.

'Do you want to give them the banana?' I ask Luna, and hand her one of the little bananas we've just bought at the till for ten baht.

Luna shrugs. That means no in Luna-speak, but I've decided she's got to be a bit braver with animals. Australia will be heaving with animals, I've read, and it's a shame if your child doesn't dare come out of the camper because a friendly kangaroo has turned up at the breakfast table.

'Go on,' I say, 'just give the banana to the monkey.'

'Are you sure?' whispers Rose. 'I don't think this place is all that professio—'

'Oooooooowwwww!!!'

The monkey thought this was all taking a bit too long, and has plunged his teeth into the banana. And into my shocked daughter's finger. Luna screams her head off.

Blood gushes from the finger.

Rose is the first to recover.

'Dan, your T-shirt!'

'Why are you making a bloody fuss about a T-shi . . . ?'

'Take your T-shirt off! Wrap it around her finger!'

I take off my T-shirt, bind it around Luna's hand, pick her up and start running. I have no idea where I'm running to. Actually thinking isn't so easy when your daughter is screaming with pain.

'Help! Help!' I yell in panic.

Rose looks around.

'Over there! Over there!' she cries, 'that man in uniform over there!'

My daughter in my arms, I grab a Thai attendant.

He laughs as he sees us coming.

'Yes, suh, what can I do faw you?' he asks in a friendly voice, before he sees the T-shirt, by now drenched with blood.

'Come! Fihst Aid?' he shouts and points urgently towards a small building near the ticket booths. We run like mad. Out of the corner of my eye I see two Japanese tourists getting their cameras ready.

A little later we stand panting (Rose and I) and screaming (Luna) in a little room behind the ticket booths. I carefully peel the T-shirt from Luna's finger. Under the blood-soaked material we see an open flesh wound. I quickly look away. Cancer didn't look as bad as this.

The Thai fetches a first-aid box from a cupboard and routinely wraps a bandage around the finger.

'Ospitaah in town. Fife minute fom heah,' he says comfortingly. 'No ploblem.'

I'd love to know what things have to look like before a Thai says there *is* a problem.

Six

Koh Samui Hospital is a modern building that looks completely trustworthy at first glance. More trustworthy than the Sint Lucas Hospital anyway. And it's white. That's always encouraging. Hospitals are supposed to be white.

▶ In Dan's view Carmen was misdiagnosed and appallingly badly treated by the Sint Lucas Hospital, and later transferred to the Antoni van Leeuwenhoek, a research hospital specializing in the treatment of cancer patients.

'Will you wait here?' I ask Rose very quietly.
'Are you sure?'
'Yes.'
In the First Aid consulting room I hold on tight to my daughter. I press her even more tightly to me as the doctor prepares a syringe.
'Ow – Ow – Oowowow!'
Trails run down Luna's cheeks as the needle goes into her finger. I remember the injection in Carmen's hand before each chemo treatment. Now, as then, I wish I could bear the pain for her, but once more I can only hold on tight to Luna's hand.

I'll take good care of your daughter, the words buzz round my head. If I'd only listened to Rose, this wouldn't have happened, damn it. What am I doing here anyway, on this stupid island with its bloody palm-trees and idiotic bloody monkeys? Why leave Amsterdam? No one would have dreamed of biting Luna's finger there. And now we we're going to Australia, with all the snakes, scorpions, crocodiles and deadly insects.

'I begin. You howd huh hand.'

I see him picking up a needle and thread. I hold Luna's hand firm and tight, and see the fear in her eyes, eyes looking at me with a Papa-why-is-your-face-so-blank expression. *I'll take good care of your daughter.* Next thing we'll find out the monkey has some sort of disease. Fuck – doesn't HIV come from monkeys? I look at Luna's face as the man stitches her up. She's white as a sheet.

The doctor nods. 'I'm leddy.'

'The doctor's finished, darling.' I stroke Luna's cheek.

She barely reacts.

'Monkey fom Monkey Fahm?'

I nod.

'Fahm no good. Dangeous. She has to have fouh moh injection.'

I'm not going to translate that.

'Evey week. Against labias.'

Labias?? I'll look it up later on the Internet.

'And, erm – Doctor – Is it possible the monkey had, erm – HIV?'

The doctor laughs. 'No. That only when fucky-fucky.'

■

Rose runs up to us and hugs us as we come out of the door of the First Aid block.

I hide my head in the hollow of her shoulder and spontaneously start crying.

'Come on, darling,' says Rose. 'Come on . . .'

Seven

'Luna, look, planes with kangaroos on them!'

'Where, where?' she cries excitedly.

I lift her up and show her. 'There! On the planes, do you see them?'

I point with my arm along her eye-line towards the Qantas planes that stand outside the departure gates in Terminal 2 at Bangkok Airport.

Luna peers along my pointing arm and nods enthusiastically. With her monkey-finger, which has a fat bandage wrapped round it, she points to a Boeing 767.

'Is that big one our plane?'

'I think so,' I nod, and find I'm just as childishly excited as my three-year-old daughter.

Rose does her best to laugh along enthusiastically.

'In a few days we might see real kangaroos!'

'Real kangaroos?'

Luna eyes me suspiciously.

'Yes.'

'So they really exist?'

That's what you get from living in the city.

I nod.

'And do they bite?'

On the flight yesterday from Koh Samui to Bangkok and the taxi ride to our hotel, Luna was as stoned as an Italian tourist in an Amsterdam coffee-shop. After that she woke up for a while, over dinner in the Sukhothai, the most luxurious hotel in Bangkok, where I'd treated the three of us after all the misery. The Sukhothai is an oasis of loveliness on a sixteen-lane highway in Bangkok. The only thing a person has to do there is breathe, eat, drink and shit.

From the moment Luna fell asleep again, Rose and I lay on the bed talking. I'd ordered a bottle of Dom Pérignon from room service, and apologized for the last few days. Rose said that was a relief, because she'd begun to think she was only there to help dispel any remaining doubt that 'Dan & Rose' were over and done with. She laughed loudly, like she'd just told a good joke, and said she wanted to go to bed with me now. At least – if I was interested. I said my interest was firm and upstanding, and it was a good thing I'd booked a family suite with a separate room for Luna.

■

Our plane leaves in an hour. Rose is spending another five days in Bangkok before she goes back to Amsterdam. She wants to book a cheap guesthouse somewhere, and then see what happens, she said. She might do some tourist things. The Grand Palace, the floating market, the Jim Thompson House.

We walk to the bar in Terminal 2. It's an English pub with carpets on the floor, a lot of dark wood and a group of noisy men in XXXL T-shirts. I order a Guinness for myself, a bottle of water for Rose, an apple juice and a bag of crisps for Luna.

I feel Rose watching me as I walk towards the bar. As I'm waiting for my order, I look behind me. Luna is sitting open-mouthed listening to her cassette of fairy tales. Sometimes she grins. I see Rose watching her expressionlessly.

Another fifty minutes. I start counting the minutes like I used to at school, in German class.

I come back with the drinks and the crisps.

'Mmmm!' cries Luna from under her headphones. 'Crisps!'

I burst out laughing. Rose doesn't react.

'The Guinness is delicious.'

'. . .'

'Want a sip?'

'No.'

'Not even a tiny sip?'

She shakes her head irritably.

Another three-quarters of an hour.

I read the writing on the back of the crisp packet.

Forty minutes.

The Walkman clicks off.

'Pap, can you turn over the tape?'

'Of cour— Erm, you know, why not listen later on? That'll be friendlier, because Rose is still here.'

Luna starts sulking.

I give her a look of rebuke. 'Luna . . .'

Thirty-five minutes.

'When you wake up tomorrow in the plane, you'll be in Australia,' says Rose.

Luna nods.

'Are you looking forward to it?'

Luna nods violently. Rose turns back towards me.

148

I see it's hard for her. Quick, change the subject. 'And what about you? Looking forward to your extra few days?'

'Sure,' she says stoutly.

Half an hour.

'And will you go to the floating market?'

'I don't know. If I feel like it. I think I'll see if there are any nice people in the guesthouse, and maybe go out.'

'Good idea,' I wink. 'You might find a nice boyfriend.'

'Very funny.'

Twenty-five minutes. First we fly to Darwin and then on to Cairns. Pick up the camper up there, and then on to Port Douglas.

I take another look at the travel-agency brochure. 'Where the rainforest meets the reef,' it says. The Great Barrier Reef is less than an hour's drive away. In the photograph, the jungle is separated from the sea only by a snow-white stretch of sand, Four Mile Beach.

Twenty minutes. My excitement is mounting by the minute, unbridled optimism. Now everything's going to sort itself out. Papa & Luna. Camper. Freedom. Peace. Space. No women. Beach bars better than anything in Bloemendaal. Barbecues. Kangaroos. I stuff the brochure back in my bag.

Fifteen min— 'Attention, passengers for flight QF204 to Darwin, your flight is now ready for boarding, please proceed to gate D-6.'

'I – erm – think we'd better go.'

We walk towards the door.

'There. Gate D. By that door.'

We walk towards two great massive sliding doors. Light beige, with flaking paint. Like there's a rubbish dump on the other side rather than a gate to Australia. Why aren't they just made of glass, like they are in Schiphol, so parting doesn't seem so final?

We stop a few yards from the doors. Rose looks sad. Luckily she isn't crying.

'So – erm – that's that, then,' I begin.

I hug her. We kiss. She opens her mouth. The last time I'll taste her tongue. She holds my head tightly and twists her tongue around mine. Slowly she lets me go. I laugh.

'Cool kiss.'

She forces a smile. 'Good luck – together.'

Luna lifts her arms in the air. Rose picks her up. 'Bye, lovey – you'll be good for Papa?'

'Yes.'

Luna and I walk hand in hand towards the sliding door. We turn round one last time. I blow a kiss. 'Bye . . .'

'Bye – bon voyage!'

'I'll email you.'

Rose shakes her head. Then Luna and I walk through the paint-flaked sliding door towards the gate.

Just before the door slides shut, I look behind me and catch a last glimpse of a waving Rose.

The last remnant of Amsterdam is deleted.

Part Three

Dan & Luna

We have all the time in the world
Time enough for life to unfold
All the precious things life has in store
And we got all the love in the world
And as time goes by you will find we need nothing more
And we got all the time in the world for love
Nothing more, nothing less, only love
Only love

Fun Lovin' Criminals, from 'We Have All the Time in the World'
(*Mimosa*, 1999)

One

As an ex-adman I should have known: things always look nicer in brochures.

The guy who escorts us to the car park points at something sitting between two enormous camper-vans. Ours looks like it hasn't had enough to eat.

I check the documents from the travel agents back home, but this is really it. A Nissan camper-van. 1.69 m by 4.5 m by 2.5 m. Outside measurements. Carmen has more room where she is.

As I climb in after the man into our Smurfmobile, I bump my head. He laughs. 'Ya o'right, mate?'

No, you shit-face, if I'd known this was going to be our caravan for the next few months, I'd have signed up for an evening class in Quasimodo. And that's taking into consideration there's a house standing empty in Amsterdam Oud Zuid with four hundred square metres and a ceiling four metres high.

I'm too tired to go back and ask if there are any other campers available that weren't built with Smurfs or Japanese people in mind. Perhaps I'll get used to it. The guy explains how the seats fold down to make the sleeping area, and shows me the gas and water pipes. I nod and nod. Luna stands yawning next to the camper, rubbing her bandaged monkey-finger against her cheek. Soon she won't even need Poppy to go to sleep with.

With that, the guy throws me the keys and a 'G'day, mate!' I sling in our suitcases, lift Luna into the cabin and then climb in on the other side.

The steering wheel is missing.

Red-faced, I switch places with Luna and try to get out of the man's sight a.s.a.p. In the rear-view mirror I see him shaking his head as he watches after me.

Then off we go. Papa the clown and Mamaluna.

Two

Wherever the British have set foot on dry land, they've screwed everything up with this issue of driving on the left. It's lethal.

Fortunately we soon leave the morning rush hour of Cairns behind us. The sun is shining brightly, and the journey to Port Douglas is gorgeous. The road twists along cliffs and ravines. With a quick glance to the side, I note that the sea lies tens of metres below us. Luna doesn't see anything. After a few minutes she's fallen asleep. In the plane she must have slept for six or seven hours at most.

The time difference is starting to take its toll on me, too, I notice. Another ten kilometres. I bite the inside of my cheek to stay awake, open the window, tense my thigh muscles till they hurt and give myself little slaps on the cheek.

I consider the creep at the customs desk. No doubt at the campsite we'll have to fill out more Australian forms, then we have to transform this thing into something resembling a bedroom. It feels more like work than play.

I stretch. A shower wouldn't be too bad right now, I smell like a mouldy polecat and my mouth tastes like a lizard has been crapping in it for the last few hours.

At last. Welcome to Port Douglas. 'Where the rainforest

meets the reef.' I start feeling OK again. Tomorrow or the day after, Danny-Boy's going to be in the Reef.

Carm was twenty-five when she came here. In one of the photographs I've brought with me she's posing in a diving suit on a boat. I haven't looked at it since we got on the plane in Holland. This whole Australia trip is already a nine on the pilgrimage scale. Anyway the picture's burned into my memory. Even in that diving suit, you can see what divine breasts she had. According to her tried and tested principle, her zip is pulled down to display a considerable portion of her fabulous curves to the public. She looks extraordinarily luscious in the picture, and two whopping great nipples are poking out through the diving suit. There's a little emblem on the suit with a name that begins with a P, I discovered with a magnifying glass. On Google I've discovered a diving club in Port Douglas called Poseidon Reef Adventures. Maybe that's it. In the photograph Carmen is standing beside two boys and a girl. Carm's holding her diving mask in one hand. In the other she nonchalantly holds a cigarette between her fingers. She smoked from the age of fifteen until the day she was diagnosed with cancer. Even the way she used to light her cigarette would turn me on, though I don't smoke myself. If we were in the car and Carmen was driving, it was a particularly fantastic ritual. First she'd open the window a crack, then push in the cigarette lighter on the dashboard. Then – always in this order – she'd pick up the pack of Marlboro Lights – later, when the cancer had spread and she'd taken up smoking again, it was ordinary Marlboros – tap the bottom of the pack a few times with her index finger, extract a ciggy with her lips, remove the hot lighter from the dashboard, light the ciggy as it was suspended from her wonderfully full lips, inhale while sticking the cigarette-lighter-thing back in the dashboard. And then – when she had a hand free – would come the moment I'd been anticipating when she'd first picked up the pack: she'd take the cigarette out of her mouth between her index and middle fingers, turn her face slightly to the left, keeping her eyes on the road, and blow the smoke in the direction of the open window. Fantastic. What a woman!

In the passenger seat Luna has woken up. In a whiny voice she says she doesn't feel very well. Her face is white. It can't be anything to do with the monkey-finger. That had stopped hurting on the plane here, she said.

She couldn't be getting car-sick? Luckily we've only got about another six and a half thousand kilometres still to drive.

Three

Luna sits like a dead bird on the bench in reception at the Four Mile Drive Camper-Van Park. She's even put her fairy-tales Walkman down beside her.

The lady at reception gives me a map and, with a fluorescent yellow pen, highlights the spot where we can plonk our Smurfmobile. It isn't far from reception and the swimming pool.

She asks if there's anything else I need. I reply that I could use a bottle of water and that I'll be back later to pick up information on rental bikes, opening hours of the Rainforest Habitat Wildlife Sanctuary and, of course, scuba diving on the Reef. With a nod to Luna I make it clear that I have other priorities right now. I take the bottle of water and the map, pick up Luna and trudge to our mobile kennel. Christ, it's boiling. I'm sweating like a typhoid victim.

'Do we have to do any more driving?' Luna sulks when we're outside.

'Just a little tiny bit. Do you want to sit on Papa's lap? Then you can help me drive.'

It works. A little smile appears on her face.

We drive across the camping ground at a walking pace. Not that we need to, because it's quiet here.

Very quiet.

Outside the toilet blocks a little Asian woman is scrubbing the washbasins, and she's the only other person I can see. High season is clearly over for the Four Mile Drive Camper-Van Park.

I look at the map. Number 17. On the wooden poles indicating the camper plots I see that we're at number 14. They could just as well have put us at number 1, but perhaps the plots have already been booked for the weekend. Yes, I'm sure it'll be busier tomorrow.

Each camper plot is equipped with a concrete slab covering several square metres. For a moment I'm not sure whether to park our vehicle on top of it or next to it. There's actually another camper parked a little further along. It's parked next to the slab. I decide to follow its example. Still no idea what the concrete is for, though.

In ten minutes I've transformed the seats into a sofa bed for two people, observed by a pallid Luna. I take the sheets that the man from Britz Car Rental gave me out of their plastic packaging and bump my head again, this time on the tailboard, which I've opened up so that I can make up the beds from outside.

Yawning already, Luna lets me undress her. It's the middle of the day, and I wouldn't be at all surprised if it was forty degrees in our little bread-bin. I give Luna a kiss, take a folding chair out from under the sofa bed and go and sit on the concrete terrace. Peace at last.

I contentedly put the bottle of water to my mouth and look at the void around me.

'Papa?' comes a voice from inside the camper.

Sigh.

'Where's my dummy? And Poppy?'

I wish she'd never been given Poppy. I stand up and climb back into our little box. Luckily I know where I've left these bare necessities: in the hand luggage. This, I discover after a quarter of an hour's search and a phone call later, is still on the counter of Britz Car Rental at Cairns Airport.

■

They'll hold the bag for us for a week, when Luna and I pass through Port Douglas again on our way south to Cairns.

From what I could hear, the man didn't quite understand our route planning, but I could hardly tell him I'd gone to Port Douglas specially to see the diving club where my late wife had spent a day sitting on a boat ten years ago.

Fortunately my supply of dummies is big enough to lose one here and there. And when I tell Luna that I have – thanks to Anne – brought along a reserve Poppy, she thinks I'm a Super-Papa. She manages a smile on her corpse-white face, and gives me a grin, too. Then she takes Poppy II in her arms as if Poppy I had never existed. She must get that from me, I think.

Four

One of the most undignified ways of being woken up, and one that Amnesty International never mentions, is by a wailing child's voice a few inches away from your ear.

I'm lying next to Luna on the sofa bed. Peeping at my watch, I see we've been asleep for less than half an hour. You can shut out most human misery, or at least drink it away, but there's no escaping a weeping child's cry, particularly when it's your own child.

It slowly dawns on me that there's something else I can't escape: a curious smell in this kitchenette. A sour, penetrating smell.

I turn over with a jerk. Luna is on her knees, sobbing. She's in a terrible state, and so are the sheets all around her. To think that so much vomit can come from a three-and-a-half-year-old child. If I hear anyone say you can't be revolted by your own child, I'll just push him head-first into a bucket of his own dear little toddler's peristaltic emissions.

■

Once I've scrubbed Luna down under the shower, I set about sorting out the camper. According to the dashboard thermometer, it's forty-two degrees. Everything is covered in it.

Sheets, Poppy, nightie, pillows, the dark-blue curtains, even the sofa bed covers haven't emerged unscathed. A big dark stain has passed through the sheets and formed on the flower-patterned seats. Brilliant!

Now we're going to drive across Australia in a doll's car that already stinks like the gates of hell – and that's after only one afternoon.

By now the neighbours in the camper further along have arrived, a couple so old I wouldn't be surprised if they'd witnessed some of the Bible stories at first hand. They give me a pitying look as I walk by with the washing, and give me some cleaning stuff consisting of a mop, a bottle of all-purpose cleaner and a little cup of washing powder. The woman tells me Luna's doll and the covers can go in the washing machine. When I come back from the wash-house, I see them quickly bringing their clothes in. Menacing greyish-green clouds are drifting into the sky above the Four Mile Drive Camper-Van Park.

Five

Luna and I play countless games of the Sesame Street Memory Game in our kitchenette, which now smells strongly of all-purpose cleaner. Every few minutes I look suspiciously out the window to see if the tropical downpour outside is showing any signs at all of stopping.

Just as night begins to fall, the rain eases off. We can forget Port Douglas tonight. I read Luna a story and tuck her in, with sarongs and towels as substitute bedclothes.

I manage to explain to her that my packing didn't take account of the possibility of the loss of two dolls. Even though she hasn't eaten a thing since breakfast on the plane this morning, she isn't feeling hungry, she says, and coincidentally I agree with her. I wouldn't have known what to give her. Even the bag of lollipops was confiscated by the customs man. Our entire supplies consist of a bottle of luke-warm water.

As soon as it seems the rain has stopped, I get out of the camper and walk a little way across the campsite. Even after the storm it's incredibly hot. I still haven't even showered, it occurs to me. What I'd really like to do is jump into the pool for a bit. Perhaps the neighbours would be willing to look after Luna for a little while.

I walk to their camper and knock on the front door.

They're not there.

There isn't a soul on the whole site.

What the fuck am I doing here in a camper-van park, deserted but for a pair of old wrinklies, at the back end of Australia, completely alone with my daughter, who's been sick on the first day after a three-quarter-of-an-hour drive? Couldn't I have found a bolthole somewhere closer to home? Only New Zealand and the moon are further away. That's some advice Nora gives out. She really thinks I'm like the guy in *The Alchemist*, about to cross the whole goddamn desert in search of symbolic messages, huh? Let's just think about that.

So, am I supposed to wait for some old guy with a revolting beard and a painted face to tell me cryptically where the key to happiness and wisdom is? And then I'll be handed a book that'll make me see the light? Or am I supposed to act natural and keep my eye out for a decrepit beach club that just happens to be for sale because the ninety-six-year-old owner passed away last winter, and then, utilizing my innate talents, settle down and work here, awaiting fulfilment of the prediction for Luna and me, the one where 'The Woman Who Is Going to Change My Life' – with whom I'm going to make Australian brothers and sisters for Luna – will suddenly pop up? Sure, yeah, why don't I just instruct Anne and Thomas to sell the house, and for the next thirty years we'll celebrate Christmas at thirty degrees in the shade.

Christ, I don't even want to think about it. If it's as quiet as this everywhere, I'd rather head for Byron Bay, 'Australia's No. 1 love-and-peace spot', which Carmen waxed so lyrical about in her photograph album.

I look at the map. Byron Bay is another cool two and a half thousand kilometres to the south.

Six

I wake up in our little microwave at half past seven in the morning.

Luna's eyes are still shut. She looks very sweet like that. I kiss her gently on the forehead and stroke her cheek for a moment. She's fast asleep. Now I can finally go to reception for a moment and see if they've got anything to eat and drink.

'Hello,' the lady says affably. 'How's your little daughter?'

'Not too good. She isn't used to the heat yet.'

I ask her how far it is to the centre of Port Douglas, whether I can rent a bike, where I could find a doctor who knows something about rabies, which scuba-diving companies she can recommend and whether she can offer us anything to eat and drink.

She has good news.

Apparently we can cycle along the beach the whole four miles from the camp to Port Douglas. The place is packed with companies that organize diving trips to the Reef, and tomorrow morning, Sunday, there's live music in most of the pubs.

The bad news is that it really is low season. Next week there won't be a soul here, we're in North Queensland and the rainy season is just around the corner, which is why there's no one in the van park. So she can't help me with company, either my age or Luna's, she says with a smile, or with teabags for that matter, but she does have a stack of brochures for scuba-diving trips, a pack of crackers and jam, a bag of crisps, two bottles of ice-cold Fosters, an all-terrain bike with a child's seat and two helmets. 'Queensland law,' she says with a smile as she hands me two helmets. I look at them. Forget it. Luna can do what she likes, but I'm not going cycling tomorrow looking like a numpty.

From reception I cycle to the wash-house in the toilet block. I get the washing out of the machine and hang Poppy, Luna's nightie, the sheets and the sarong on the washing line beside the wash-house.

Luna is just waking up as I get to the camper. She has put her dummy in her mouth and, in the absence of Poppies I and II, is rubbing her monkey-finger over her cheek.

'Morning, sweetie. I expect you're hungry?'

She nods. She seems to be feeling a bit better.

A little later we're sitting at a folding table beside our dinky toy eating crackers and jam. Luna is only taking little bites, but at least she's eating. I've put on some tea. The neighbours did have teabags.

Luna looks enthralled at the foam-rubber helmet with the picture of Snoopy. I tell her we're going to cycle along the beach today. I decline to mention we're going there to see a doctor who's going to take off the caked bandage and give her a rabies injection. Even though a child seat isn't exactly the sexiest thing in the world, the mountain bike just about gets away with it, and does so completely when Luna is sitting on it. In the little mirror on the cupboard door of the

166

camper I show her how grown-up she looks in her Snoopy helmet, bright-pink sunglasses and the hippest summer dress from her suitcase. Papa is helmetless, but wearing a smart pair of sunglasses and a casually faded T-shirt from the Melkweg.

You never know, perhaps we'll bump into 'The Woman Who Is Going to Change My Life' today, in the doctor's waiting room, at one of the diving companies or just, as you might expect, in a pub or a beach-club. If so, you'd want to be looking pretty smart.

Seven

It's called Four Mile Beach, and the name seems to fit.

Miles of white sand, with the edge of a dense forest on one side and the sea on the other. You can cycle on the sand along the coast, the receptionist said; all we have to do is head north and we'll end up in Port Douglas. We've got a doctor's appointment there, for Luna's injection.

When we get to the beach via the path through the forest, I look around slightly anxiously. The receptionist had told me that Four Mile Beach was perfectly peaceful, but there are limits. There isn't a single soul in sight. Let alone 'The Woman Who Is Going to Change My Life'. I might as well have worn a Teletubbie suit.

Hmmm. So let's lie on the beach for a bit. I'd like to take a dip in the sea with Luna, but I can't, the receptionist said. At this time of year it's full of box jellyfish, one sting of which can be fatal. Especially for children.

There's one section that is cut off from the sea with fine-meshed nets, so that you can swim safely. OK, but it might be better to wait and see what the doctor's going to say about the injury to Luna's finger before going in the water.

I pick up my rucksack, spread the sarong out on the sand and help Luna out of her dress. No point putting on sun-cream; after a week in Koh Samui she's already as brown as Judith Chalmers.

After lying in the sun for half an hour, I reckon I've seen all that I'm going to. Luna is playing listlessly in the sand with a twig. She doesn't exactly look radiant with pleasure. I'm just looking around in search of proof that there's life on this planet. *Nada.* This whole low-season business is really going to get on my tits. What I'd like to do today is meet some people I can talk to about something other than the washability of sofa-bed cushions and the Sesame Street Memory Game. Ideally in a nice beach bar. The landscape's magnificent, but it's also nice to have a drink to hand.*

Cycling time.

I pack our things away and tell Luna we're going. I lift her into the child seat and push the bike through the powdery sand along the sea. It's half past eleven, and the sun is really beating down on us. What am I doing? This is harder work than I've done in months.

'Keep going, Pap,' Luna says encouragingly. 'You're nearly there.'

I look back and see Luna sitting like a princess on her child seat with her Snoopy helmet and her sunglasses. Then I burst out laughing.

What am I complaining about? Hordes of young parents would give up their jobs to come here with their offspring. This is what they're always going on about in *Parenting* magazine. Quality time with the kids. Come on. This is what I escaped Amsterdam to do. Just enjoy it, you twat!

---

* Freely wrampled from the Dutch poet Willem Kloos (1859–1938), not that I'm an expert on the man's oeuvre, but a bit of googling works wonders.

I look at Luna. 'So you want to go to the sea, princess?'

She nods.

Suddenly I start shrieking like a baboon and run towards the sea, pushing the bike. Luna roars with laughter. 'No, no, not into the sea!' she cries.

'Yes, into the sea,' I yell back. I only stop when I'm up to my ankles in the water. My daughter is nearly wetting herself. I open my eyes exaggeratedly wide and stick my finger in the air in the Mr Bean gesture Carmen always used when she'd just had a ridiculous idea.

'Welcome to the water-bike, your highness,' I say in an exaggerated voice. I jump on and ride the bike through the waves and honk like a ship's horn. We're going faster and faster, with our wheels in the surf. The warm sea-water splashes up, Luna stretches her arms wide, tilts her head back into the wind and shouts.

'Faster, Pap, faster!'

I utter primal howls, pedal a bit harder and cycle a bit further into the water. It's as if we're riding through a car wash. In no time we're both soaked to the skin, and in my case it's from sweat more than the spraying water.

Eight

They certainly don't skimp with the meat here. What a hamburger!

'We just cut off his ears, wipe his ass and serve up the beast,' it says on the menu, and it's no word of a lie. Even Tash wouldn't have been able to take this piece of meat in all at once.

We're sitting in the Iron Bar, a cafe with a decor of corrugated iron, rusty oil-cans and bits of tools I don't recognize. Presumably it's supposed to represent the outback, because I also see cacti, a wittily intended 'No Shooting' board with bullet-holes in it and a dilapidated road sign saying that the distance from here to New York is 9,441 miles, and even to Tokyo it's a cool 4,519 miles.

In a few days there are going to be Toad Races here, it says on a blackboard. They've drawn a frog beside it, so I work out that 'toads' must mean frogs.

'Luna, do you want to see a frog race?'

'What's that?'

'A few frogs seeing who the fastest frog is.'

She looks at the drawing of the frog on the board.

'Will we go together?'

I nod.

'Then I want to go.'

The hamburger tastes fantastic. I've just downed an ice-cold bottle of Fosters in one go and – 'Wannanuthawan, mate?' – already there's another right in front of my nose. I've just taught Luna to say 'Cheers, big ears' when she raises her glass, because Mama always used to do it when she started getting pissed. Luna thinks it's funny too, because now we have to shout 'Tjiers-bik-iers!' before every sip. Her bottle of orange juice is already three-quarters empty, so it's quite a success from the educational point of view as well. Now she's scooping ice-cream out of a coupe the size of a champagne cooler. The child herself is barely visible behind it.

Yes, this is more like it, this is a holiday.

She had more than deserved the ice-cream. I was unbeliev-ably proud of my daughter at the doctor's just now. No tears when the bandage came off. It still didn't look very attractive. She can't swim for the next few days, the doctor said. When the anti-rabies injection went in, three little 'ows' came out of Luna's mouth. And that was it. Massive great thing it was. I had to blink away a tear when I saw the face she pulled.

Outside I picked her up, spun her around and told her how tough she'd been and what a fantastically sweet and beautiful and clever and wonderful and super-duper-fluper brilliant kid she was.

And that this afternoon we weren't going to go to the diving club that Papa so much wanted to go to, but there'll be another chance later this week.

Plenty of time.

Nine

At a chemist's in Port Douglas we buy Luna a supply of travel tablets for the journey from here to Kangaroo Island. Intrigued, I look at a poster showing a strange bird and the words 'Slip! Slop! Slap!' It could be the title of a porn film featuring Ron Jeremy, but I find out from the pretty girl behind the counter that the words are part of a campaign to persuade parents always to make their children *slip* on a shirt, *slop* on sun-cream and *slap* on a hat. As she explains this, she looks at Luna, who, in spite of a week in Thailand, got her shoulders slightly burned on yesterday's bike-ride. I get a folder thrust into my hands, with a statistic showing that several thousand Australians die of skin cancer every year.

This is enough to make me buy a big bottle of factor-36 sun-cream for Luna, and the kind of UV-resistant wetsuit that I've already seen a few toddlers walking around in.

I ask the girl in the shop if she happens to know if there's a little church in Port Douglas. She says there are about five. I take out of my rucksack the photograph showing Carmen standing beside a white church.

'Ah, St Mary's by the Sea,' she laughs. She tells me there's a little park at the end of the street, right beside the sea. That's where it is.

We cycle towards the little park. When we get there I recognize it straight away. A little white wooden church, just by the sea. I show Luna the photograph of Mama. The only difference is that the trees in the background have grown. By the look of it, the photograph was taken just by the entrance. We cross the lawn. Yes. Around about here. I ask Luna if she wants to pose where Carmen stood. When I look through the lens I can't help swallowing. At the same time I'm a bit embarrassed with myself. What am I actually trying to do with this photograph? I'm like a groupie. Let's go inside for a moment, now that we're here. Either you're a tourist or you aren't.

Inside we see the sea through the open window. Hey, a church with sea views. Good bait for customers.

Luna is more impressed by the pictures and paintings than the view. I follow her eyes. Jesus carrying the cross, Jesus on the cross, not exactly cheerful stuff. I look around for a painting showing the happier side of human life, and point to one at the back of the church, in which Joseph and Mary and the three kings and everybody stand looking at the little fellow in the crib. A baby with a halo around his head strikes me as better for the delicate soul of a child than a man with nails through his feet and a crown of thorns on his head.

I tell Luna the story of the birth in Bethlehem.

'Is Mary Jesus's Mama?'

I nod.

'And who's his Papa?'

'Erm . . . actually God is Jesus's Papa. Have you ever heard of God?'

Luna nods and looks at the painting again. I see her eyes scanning the whole thing. 'Why isn't God there?'

'He lives in ... in heaven. No one knows exactly what God looks like.'

Luna studies the painting intensely. I see her looking at a point above the stable.

'Who are those fat babies with the wings?'

'They're angels, darling,' I laugh.

She looks at me in disbelief. 'Isn't Mama an angel, too?'

I tell her that even grown-ups don't know what angels really look like, and that painters mostly show them with wings, because angels come down from heaven every now and again to help us, just as Mama helps us from time to time.

As I hear myself talking, it all sounds too ludicrous for words and Luna doesn't look entirely sure, either. 'Mama is much bigger than those angel babies. Perhaps those little angels there ...' – she points to the painting – 'are babies who have died.'

I put a coin in the little box and let Luna take a candle. With her tongue sticking out of her mouth, she holds the candle in one of the flames. We put it among the other candles.

'If we're quiet now and close our eyes,' I whisper, 'it'll be easier for us to think of Mama, and then it'll be a bit like she's with us.'

Luna nods.

We close our eyes and fall silent.

I don't care for churches much, but I have to admit this place feels good. The devotion, the silence, the peace and the candle – it really is as if we're closer to Carm. I open my eyes and look at Luna, who still has her eyes closed.

'Have you finished?' I whisper.

She shakes her head. 'Again!' she says resolutely, with her eyes closed.

I fall silent again.

'Shall we say something to Mama?' I ask after a while.

'Yes!'

I look around me for a moment. There's no one else in the church. I clear my throat and begin in a quiet voice. 'Hello, Mama ... We're in Australia now, in a church that you've been to as well, and we're having a lovely time together ... But ...'

I wait for a moment. It hurts to express it like this.

'But ... we ... miss you. Will you think of us in heaven and ... take good care of us?'

I open my eyes and dry them quickly before Luna sees. She's still keeping her eyes shut. Her mouth is open.

'Luna?'

She opens her eyes.

'Are you coming?'

She nods and takes my hand.

As we're walking out of the church she looks around again for a moment.

She waves and blows a kiss.

Ten

The Poseidon Reef Adventure Centre is covered with loads of photographs of brilliantly coloured corals, fish for which the Creator let his imagination run riot, and happily waving divers.

Carmen isn't up there.

'G'day, mate,' says a tanned boy with Oakley sunglasses in his sun-bleached hair. He has a leather bootlace around his neck with a shark-tooth hanging from it. Around his wrist he wears a collection of coloured bead bracelets and a watch on which you can tell, when you're three hundred metres under water, what time it is on the moon. An impressive tattoo emerges from the sleeves of his T-shirt.

'Hey, man,' I say in my most nonchalant tone, 'can you give me some information about scuba diving?'

'You've come to the right address, mate!' the boy says brightly. I ask him where the company's diving spots are. The Great Barrier Reef is no more than a stone's throw from here, after all. That's why it's also possible to make two or three dives at various locations in the Outer Reef, the most beautiful part of the reef, in a single day. I flick through the brochure showing the various possibilities and decide to go for the most comprehensive trip with three dives, including hire of the diving equipment and lunch with freshly killed fish. Tomorrow morning at six in the harbour.

I nod. As the boy fills in the forms, I ask him how long they've been going.

'Almost five years.'

Oh. So this wasn't Carmen's diving club. Shall I ask if there's another one beginning with P . . . ?

'Why?'

'My wife was here once,' I want to reply, but it sounds a bit weak. Carmen's diving club probably closed long ago. 'Nothing. Just curious.'

The boy has finished the paperwork, and asks me if I want to settle up now.

I take my credit card and ask if I have to pay anything else for my daughter. I point to Luna, who is staring engrossed at a picture of a happy little fish with orange and white stripes that looks as if it's a supporter of the Dutch football team.

'Oh, will your little daughter be joining you, mate?'

'Of course.'

'And your wife?'

Hey, we were getting on so well. 'I don't have a wife.'

'But who's going to look after your daughter when you're diving, then?'

I tell him that Luna's very easy. If someone on board can keep an eye on her while I'm in the water, it'll all be fine, because I know my child well enough.

The boy shakes his head so hard that his shark-tooth bangs back and forth.

'We can't do that, mate.'

'What do you mean, you can't do that?' I ask, but I can see trouble on its way.

'Queensland law, mate. Children aboard must be accompanied by at least one parent or adult.'

'C'mon, man, please . . .' I implore.

■

Half an hour later, after trying in vain to book with Haba Dive & Snorkel and Calypso Reef Charters I finally seek advice from the Tourist Office.

They have a bright idea.

A short time later I'm the proud owner of two tickets for the Captain Nemo Experience. Tomorrow, Papa and Luna are going to see the most beautiful coral reefs and fishes in the world in the *Sesame Street* version.

A glass-bottomed boat.

Even from here, I can hear them laughing in Amsterdam.

Eleven

I look at my watch. Half past two in the morning. I haven't had a wink of sleep. Earlier this evening we couldn't get into the Iron Bar. In the evening, children are forbidden in establishments where alcohol is served. I'm getting pretty fed up with all this Queensland law stuff.

I gently open the door of the camper and go and sit outside on one of the camping chairs. Near the toilet block I see a light burning, further away it's pitch-dark. The only sign of life is the sound of the crickets. Bah! I crave the sounds of the city at night. Line 16 heading back to the depot. Students who have just rolled out of De Gruter, waking up the whole block. The irritating moped of the morning newspaper salesman.

I want to hear human sounds. Not crickets. I stare silently into the dark void. Even our elderly neighbours left yesterday. We're completely alone now.

Port Douglas. 'Where the rainforest meets the reef.'

What misery.

And I haven't even got any beer left in the fridge. Tomorrow we'll buy another six-pack of Fosters. Christ, I'd love a beer. Or a line.

Shall I pick up a book? Oh no, then we'll have all that

nonsense with the torch again, or else I'll have to turn on the light in the camper and that'll wake up Luna. And it'll fill up with mosquitoes. A lamp. Tomorrow I'll buy a decent lamp.

Wait a minute. I could of course . . .

Hmm. No . . .

Or should I?

What time is it? Ten to three. What time does that make it in Thailand? About midnight? Hmm – could be – shall I . . .

What day is it today? Tuesday. She'll be heading off shortly. It might be nice to wish her a pleasant flight.

Of course she'd love that. And it would give me a chance to say I'm sorry I was such a dick in Bangkok.

■

Hey, damn it.

Come on, pick up.

Is she on the plane already?

■

An hour later I'm woken in the camper by the sound of an incoming text. I quickly muffle the phone under the pillow. Fortunately Luna goes on sleeping.

I look in my in-box.

> Hi! I saw I'd missed your call. I'm now in the taxi on the way to the airport. I check in straight away and fly in two hours. Those five days in BK on my own were great. Met a great couple from Newcastle and a nice guy from Dublin. X, have a great time.

A nice guy from Dublin. I delete the text irritably. Great! As soon as I turn my back, Rose is being screwed by some Bono wannabe.

Fantastic, I haven't seen a single boomerang all the time I've been here and now I get one right to the head.

I don't want to hear about Bono wannabes.

I just want to hear she misses me.

Until now, it was like Rose was still there for me a little bit. As if I had a reserve parachute that I could always use in Bangkok.

What time did that text come in? I'd say about half an hour ago. She mightn't have checked in yet. Shall I just ring her? No.

If I hear Rose's voice now, I'd probably get an acute weakening of the spine and before I know it, this whole Australian expedition – with all the fuss surrounding it – would collapse in a great heap.

I can already hear them talking in Amsterdam.

Getting Rose to come to Australia is just a few notches worse than looking at the Reef from a glass-bottomed boat.

■

On the other hand.

Over the past few days I've worked out that it was a bit reckless to come all alone with Luna. What are we going to do if I can't go diving and we can't go to a frog race in the pub? What am I trying to do here on my own? What could be wrong with Rose being here as well? Couldn't she come as a friend? She's a good friend, isn't she? In Thailand everything had to be nice because it was the official end of our relationship. So there's no question of it now. That relationship is over.

■

Jesus Christ! Less than a week ago I was as relieved as the Ajax supporters when they heard that Jan Wouters had been laid off, and now I'm thinking about bringing her over here as cool as you please, just because I'm afraid of the prospect of feeling like I do now every evening for the next few months?

You know what, I'll just send her one text back, wishing her a pleasant journey and then I'll go to sleep.

Hi goddess . . .

Yuk! Far too intimate. Keep it matter-of-fact.

Hi! And take care on your return fli

Oh, what nonsense.
I quickly tap in Rose's speed-dial number.
'. . .'
'Dan?!?'
Hmm. More surprised than happy.
'Hey.'
'Christ, are you calling from Australia? I saw that you'd called – hang on, you two are OK, aren't you?'
'Yes – we're fine.'
'You sound really dreadful . . .'
'Oh. I just don't think it's my day.'
'Why are you calling?' Her voice comes healingly through the telephone. 'There isn't anything wrong, is there?'
My stomach contracts.

I tell her everything's fine. A nice camper, pleasant people, good weather, Luna in great form and we're never not gonna go home, we won't go, we won't go, we're never not gonna go home, our mother isn't home.[*] And she's dead, too. Hahaha.

'Dan.'

I come up with some story about how things aren't going all that well, but mostly because Luna has been ill. Rose shrieks with laughter when I tell her we're going out to see the Reef in a glass-bottomed boat tomorrow, and now I hear myself saying it, I can see the funny side, too.

I don't ask whether she did it with that guy.

'Have you checked in already?'

'Yes, I'm just about to go through passport control, why?'

Too late. Why the hell didn't she ring me back straight away when she saw I'd called?

'So. Did you have a good time in Bangkok?'

'Yeah, it was great. Nice people. Sandy and Don from Newcastle, and Mark, a really funny guy from Dublin.'

OK, twist the knife, why don't you.

'Did you go out?'

'Yeah, I went with them to the Supperclub, you know, like they have in Amsterdam—' Then in English, 'Oh, yes, sorry, just a moment please – erm – Dan?'

'Yes?'

'I'll text you. It's my turn.'

'Erm . . .'

Shall I – would it be . . .

---

[*] From 'Sugar Bush', Doris Day and Frankie Lane, 1952.

'I've got to hang up now!'
Too late.
'OK! Have a nice trip!'
'See you, have a great time and a big kiss for Luna!'
'Byyyee!'
And then she hangs up.
Five minutes later I get a text.

> Sweetie, you and Luna together is how it
> should be. You don't need anyone else.
> You really don't. Not even me, however
> much it might hurt. That's fine. You can do
> it, you can both do it. I'm proud of you.
> No more texts and phone calls now. Not
> for a few months.
> X x

And that's the end of grief avoidance.

Twelve

Cairns isn't a cheerful town.

Luna and I run back through the pissing rain from the food market to our camper, which is somewhere in a car park here. We've just collected Poppy from Britz Car Rental, and done a bit of shopping at the same time.

It's half past eight in the evening and Luna's tired.

About another five blocks to our parking place, I would say.

Tonight we've booked a spot at the Coconut Caravan Park, a few kilometres outside the town. But first I'll have to see if I can find it, in the dark, in this pouring rain. And then hope that reception's still open. I've forgotten what the lady said about that on the phone. Half past nine, I think. It depends if we make it or not. Oh, fuck, and then there's making up the sofa beds in our dinky toy.

We've been here for a week, and the only moments I look back on with pleasure are that afternoon when we rode our bike along the beach and the time we went to that little church.

If I'm completely honest, up until now Australia has been one big let-down.

The trip with the Captain Nemo Experience was a drama

in itself. Luna and boats seem to be just as successful as Luna and cars. By the time we were at the Reef, and Luna was able to see the promised coloured fishies through the bottom, the poor kid had spent an hour with her head in a bucket. Sick as a dog. I did my best to cuddle her through her fits of vomiting.

I couldn't help thinking of Carm, who couldn't stand boats either. On our honeymoon on the coast of Malaysia, when we were travelling to some island that was supposed to be worth the trouble, Carmen practically puked the paint off the boat. 'Now you think you're going to die, but in a few hours you'll hope you're going to die,' said the skipper, seeing the funny side. In retrospect the man seemed to have the gift of clairvoyance. Still, better hereditary sea-sickness than breast cancer.

I feel guilty a few times every day. Perhaps Anne was right and it was madness to bring Luna here. If it isn't a car or a boat spoiling her day, a monkey or a syringe is bound to pop up and bite her.

Today's rabies injection in Cairns Hospital wasn't nice. The bandage stayed on this time. The prospect of an enormous ice-cream cone afterwards was a trick any child molester would have been proud of. I felt so sorry for Luna when the needle went back in. One more injection after this.

When we finally sat down with an ice-cream and a beer on a terrace in the centre of Cairns, another tropical rainstorm broke out. We were turned away from two pubs ('Queensla—' 'Yeah, Queensland law, I know'), and in the end we just went back to the shopping mall, where I remembered seeing a big food market. We ate quickly, badly and cheaply there, surrounded by a horde of exhausted back-packers. I don't want to sound like my father, but they could have done with a bath and a haircut, before being sent off to do some good hard work.

Carmen, you should really see us walking. Papa and Luna, far from home, through the streaming rain in a monstrosity of a town where we're not allowed in anywhere.

Why the hell did you have to get cancer? If you'd just stayed well, Luna and I wouldn't have been here, and we could have been sitting on the sofa, all three of us. Now we're walking round here getting numb with cold, and you're lying rotting under the ground. *'I want to spend my life with a girl like you,'* I sang on our wedding day, remember? I need you, damn it. Your daughter needs you.

The rain is crashing down now. We must be three blocks away from the car park.

'Come on, get on my back and we'll run,' I say to Luna.

She jumps onto my back and I start running.

When I finally reach the car park, completely out of breath, I set Luna on the ground, look for my key, open the side door of the camper, lift my daughter into it and climb in after her.

Dry at last.

Luna's teeth start chattering. I quickly undress her, rub her dry and help her put on a pair of pyjamas. She's still shivering. I get back out, grab a blanket from the bed through the tailboard and wrap her up like a mummy. Then I set her in the passenger seat.

'Bit better now?'

She nods and smiles faintly.

I take off my T-shirt and go and sit bare-chested at the

steering wheel. My jeans, my underpants, everything is soaked. I shiver when I move my feet. My socks are soaking in my shoes. I could keep fish in them.*

As I'm driving out of the car park the windows steam up. I wipe them clean with the towel. The windscreen wipers are going at top speed, but they're still not going fast enough. It's bucketing, whole stretches of road are flooded. I can't see a bloody thing with that glittering road surface. At a traffic light I look at the map of Cairns in the *Lonely Planet*. Pointless. I can't even see the street signs in this weather. Straight on, though. Didn't we drive along here this afternoon? A few blocks further the road narrows and we find ourselves in a residential area. Shit! Wrong. Three turnings later, I park the camper right under a street sign. Moody Street, I can just about read. How appropriate. Christ almighty, where are we? It looks like the industrial zone of Breda Noord rather than a town in the tropics. Can someone tell me how to get to the godforsaken Coconut Caravan Park? There isn't a soul in the street. You know, all things considered, tomorrow I'm going to hand back the camper and book a return flight. This is fucking pointless. If Luna wasn't sitting next to me, I'd be quite capable of driving this sodding camper here into a wall.

I park the car along the side of the street, get out, walk down the street a little and sit down on the kerb, stripped to the waist.

Suddenly I start howling. I throw my hands over my face and hear myself screaming, I'm going to scream this whole

---

*   Wrample from *Joe Speedboat*, Tommy Wieringa (2005).

bloody town apart. I thump the tarmac with the flats of my hands. And again. And harder. And once more. And again and again, until the pain in my chest shifts to my hands. I bring the palms of my hands to my face. To my amazement I see they're bleeding.

I stare at the back of the camper, which is thirty feet away with its engine still running. I feel a sense of calm settling over me. I take a deep breath, try to stand up without using my hands and walk to the door on Luna's side. Luckily she's still asleep, with her head half resting against the glass.

Drenched through, I walk around the car and get back in. I take off my rain-drenched trousers and throw them in the back of the camper. I pick up the towel between our seats and carefully dab my hands dry. They sting. Then I look in the rear-view mirror and head back up the street. I'll just keep driving straight on until I reach a sign. My fingers are tingling, I'm shivering with cold and I'm barely dressed, sitting there in my damp underpants. I turn the air-con off. The radio on. I recognize the latest from Fun Lovin' Criminals. *'What's the matter big boys don't cry,'* sings Huey. They certainly don't in Cairns in the pissing rain. The song fades slowly away.

At the next song my heart flips.

That intro.

That guitar.

Those drums.

That voice.

I feel the warmth flowing through my freezing body. *'I want to spend my life with a girl like you ... '* The Troggs ... *'and do all the things that you want me to ... I can tell by the way you dress that you're so refined...'* our wedding *'... baby*

baby is there no chance...' our bedroom *'... I can take you ...'* our farewell dance *'... for a last dance ... why should it be that you don't notice me ...'* Carm *'... to you across the floor my love I'll send ... I just hope and pray that I can find a way to say ... Can I dance with you ...'* Carmen *'... till that time has come and we might live as one ... Can I dance with you ...'*

'Isn't this that song that you were always playing at home, Pap?' Luna says sleepily.

Thirteen

Luna sits colouring at the little table beside the camper.

I'm collecting the towels and wet clothes from yesterday evening.

We're right by the toilet block and the wash-house.

'Papa's just going to hang up the wet clothes. Will you stay here?'

Luna nods.

With the mountain of wet clothes under my arm I walk to the washing line.

Before I hang up my trousers I check to see if my pockets are empty. I find a receipt from the food market and a few coins.

Oh, and something small in the key pocket. A pellet.

I see a rolled-up, flattened piece of silver foil in my hand.

It's travelled with us all the way from Ibiza to Australia.

I'll take good care of your daughter.

Fourteen

That night I dream about kangaroos. I'm on my way back from the Finch restaurant with Ramon. When I see Rose walking along the canal, I duck down. I only stand up again when I'm sure she can't see me. Ramon laughs at me. His face looks as if he's stuck his head in a tub of icing sugar.

We walk into a stairway where paint is flaking off the walls. There are junkies lying around us. Suddenly we're on the roof terrace of my house. There's a boxing ring. A kangaroo is jumping round in the boxing ring. Ramon grins that he'd love to fight a kangaroo. The Dollies are there, too. They're exploding with laughter, and they're completely naked. Ramon puts on a pair of boxing gloves and steps into the ring. 'Come on, then,' he calls to me. I put on a pair of boxing gloves and – trembling – step after him into the ring. The kangaroo is a good foot and a half taller than me. Ramon jumps around the startled animal. He holds his gloves up in front of his face and challenges the animal by making noises with his tongue against his palate. 'Tchk-tchk-tchk . . . tchk-tchk-tchk-tchk . . .'

Suddenly the kangaroo attacks, jumps at Ramon with its paws raised and gives him a wallop. Ramon flies out of the ring and off the roof terrace, as if in a cartoon. We hear him landing in the street with a dull thud. We bend over the edge of the roof and see that his white face is covered with blood, and that his arm is lying at a strange angle. The Dollies shriek and scream at me hysterically to finish off the kangaroo. I start crying and run downstairs to the street, glance once more at the dead Ramon, have to throw up and run away, with the Dollies screaming after me from the roof of my house that I'm a coward.

■

When I wake up, drenched in sweat, it's still dark and Luna is asleep next to me, with her dummy in her mouth. The Dollies have gone.

I get up, open the drawer under the little cupboard beside the door, reach my hand in for the bit of silver foil and take it out. Then I quietly open the door of the camper, walk barefoot through the dark to the toilet block and watch the silver paper as it flushes away.

Fifteen

By the playground of the Coconut Caravan Park there's a billboard with pictures of a kangaroo, a crocodile, a cockatoo and a koala. The animals all have a hole in their head that you can stick your head through and it looks incredibly funny in photographs, our new and (once again) elderly neighbours tell us.

Luna goes for the koala.

She's wild about koalas, even if she still hasn't seen a live one. We do the koala trick a few times together every day, with me standing with my legs wide and holding my arms up in the air at an angle, like the branches of a tree. Then Luna goes and stands on a stool or a table, climbs on top of me and yells at the top of her voice that she's a koala.

Now she's playing in the grass. I'm sitting next to her in a deckchair, reading. I started *Veronica Decides to Die*, a new Paulo Coelho. I bought it today in a bookshop in Kuranda. Kuranda is a little town near here that serves as a stopping-off point for the scenic railroad. The book kept me busy throughout the whole trip on that historic slow train, along ravines and waterfalls, and then in the cable car diagonally down through the tropical rainforest.

Am I sitting far too comfortably in Nora's chairoplane?

Am I reading too much Paulo Coelho? Am I just convincing myself Carmen is still here in some way, because I can't bear the idea she's dead? The weird thing that sums it all up: a song on Rock Radio Cairns that we played at Carmen's funeral.

And so.

'With a Girl Like You'. From 1968. I've never heard the whole song on the radio in Holland. As soon as I find myself somewhere in the vicinity of a record shop I'm going to ask if it's just been reissued in Australia, perhaps that's why it's being played.

I'm not the only one thinking about Carmen. At breakfast beside the camper this morning I suddenly got a kiss from Luna. She stood up, her mouth still half full of peanut-butter sandwich, and kissed me on the mouth. Just like that.

'You're nice, Papa,' she said.

'That's why I'm Papa,' I replied.

'I have to be extra nice to you because Mama is dead,' she said. 'Because you cry even more often than I do,' she added.

I resolve to keep my tears hidden from her more often from now on. I don't think it's good that she feels responsible for her father's well-being.

Now she's sitting contentedly playing with her dolls. 'Pap?'

'Yes?'

'When people are dead . . .'

I look up. She's made a whole procession on the grass. Poppy is lying in a little box. Poppy II and her other cuddly toys are sitting around it. 'Yes?'

'Then they can't wake up again, like Sleeping Beauty, can they?'

Gulp. 'No. I'm afraid not.'

She nods and turns her head back to her dolls. I watch out of the corner of my eye. Two toys lift the box with Poppy in it and carry it away.

'Pap, did Mama want to die?'

'What makes you think that?'

'Why did she drink that potion?'

Oh. Time to call in the Department of Educational Conversations for the Prevention of Youthful Traumas. Soon she'll think that her Mama didn't want to be her Mama any more.

'Mama didn't want to die at all. But when she was in so much pain at the end, she asked for a potion.'

'Did you think that was good?'

'Yes. Otherwise she would have died the next day, or the day after that, and she'd have been in more and more pain. I didn't want that.'

'Neither did I.'

Silence.

Luna is making the cuddly toys lower the box again, I see. The box falls over, Poppy falls out. She puts her back. The other toys and Poppy II walk away, close together.

'Sometimes I still see Mama,' Luna says all of a sudden.

'Wh – what do you mean?'

'Just when I'm asleep.'

'Then you're dreaming about Mama, darling,' I say with a smile.

'No-ho! She talks to me.'

Where's the bringing-up-children handbook? Where's the child psychologist? What's a father supposed to say to that? Agree? Disagree? Make light of it?

'But – what does Mama say?'

'That she's with us.'

Here we are. At last the kind of conversation with Luna that I could have with an adult, and I don't know what I'm supposed to say.

'I never have those dreams,' I say. I hear a hint of jealousy in my voice. In all those months I haven't dreamed once about Carmen.

'They *aren't* dreams!'

'OK, OK,' I say hastily. 'But what does she say?'

'That she's with us, I said.'

'With us – here? In Australia?'

'Yes.'

Luna says it with the self-evidence reserved for those who can count their age on the fingers of one hand.*

'Oh? And, um – what did Mama look like?'

Soon I'll be asking her if Father Christmas really exists, and if she knows how the reindeer manage to get old fat-guts up in the air on his sleigh.

'Just like Mama. But she didn't have wings.'

---

* Wrample from *The Shadow of the Wind*, Carlos Ruiz Zafón (2004).

Sixteen

The two of us have been in Australia for about a month now. The monkey-finger has healed. There are no signs of rabies. Or, recently, of Carmen. And 'The Woman Who Is Going to Change My Life' doesn't seem to me in much of a hurry.

I buy a phone card in reception at the Flying Fish Point Caravan Park. Then at least I don't have to worry that a few phone calls to Holland are going to cost me a fortune. As I walk, holding hands with Luna, to the phone box near the entrance to the campsite, I wonder who to call. I'd really like to chat to Rose, but she hasn't called or texted since Bangkok.

I don't feel like talking to Ramon.

So it's Thomas and Anne. I get Thomas on the line.

'Danny boy!'

'Hey!'

How are we? Are there any gorgeous girls walking around here?

I say irritably that I haven't time for that sort of thing, with Luna. Thomas says he thinks it's great that I'm alone there with Luna.

'They'll never be able to take that away from you, pal.'

No, but if only they would, I think, because at the same moment Luna starts whining that she's bored.

'I've got to hang up now,' I sigh. Thomas asks how much longer we're staying away. I don't dare say that every day I wonder whether I should just chuck it all in and fly home.

'Wait a minute, Dan,' says Thomas. 'Anne's yelling something –' I hear her calling that she's sent an email.

'I'm supposed to tell you that she's sent some more MAs –'

'Yes, Thomas. MAs: maternal advice.'

'Oh. OK. She's emailed you something. So if you want to check your Hotmail.'

I reply that I'll do that straight away and hang up. Then I take Luna along to the campsite shop and let her choose an ice-cream. Licking contentedly, she walks back with me to the phone box.

There are still a few dollars on my card.

Shall I give Maud a ring? Make my apologies, ask how things are going at MIU and carefully let her know that I'm off the coke.

I get a new trainee at MIU on the line. I ask if Maud's there.

'And who shall I say is calling?'

'Dan.'

'Business or private?'

'Just tell Maud Dan's on the line,' I snap.

I'm put on hold for a moment.

'You've just missed her.'

'Oh.' Shall I – OK. Come on, then. 'And, um – Frank? Is he there by any chance?'

'Another moment, please, Mr Dan.'

I'm put on hold.
'Mr Dan?'
'Yes.'
'Frank isn't here.'

Seventeen

From: Anne_and_thomas_and_the_children@chello.nl

Sent: 29 October 2001

To: Danvandiepen@hotmail.com

Hi Dan!

How are you two getting on? Everything OK? Is Luna still getting carsick? It's hard, all that driving. I asked in the chemist's, and there's a very good medication you can take, and it's available in Australia as well: Dramamine by Pfizer.

One other piece of MA: don't let her have oranges before a car journey and don't let her read. The other thing to look out for is box jellyfish, they seem to be particularly dangerous for children . . .

I click the mail away. Bye, Anne.

From: Maud@strategicandcreativemarketingagencymiu.nl

Sent: 1 November 2001

To: Danvandiepen@hotmail.com

Hi Dan

Didn't feel like talking yet, I hope you understand that.

I was furious when I heard that Rose had gone to Thailand with you.

You've duped the group again. Rose mailed me a few weeks back, she wants to talk to me. I said I'd mail her when I'm ready. Maybe I'll do it some time this week. It's not her fault, after all.

Frank has started talking to me a bit again over the past week. I've told him a hundred times how sorry I am about what happened on Ameland, but he's so hurt that you can't imagine. I'll be curious to see if the friendship ever recovers.

And stupid though it might sound: I've worked out that it's best for everyone if you're away for a while.

But I hope you're having a good time there. Give Luna a big hug from me.

Maud

Hmm. Nice to hear from you.

> **From:** Natasha@strategicandcreativemarketingagencymiu.nl
> **Sent:** 2 November 2001
> **To:** Danvandiepen@hotmail.com

Hi Dan!

How are things? Not getting bored yet? I'm certainly not LOL. It was Amsterdam Dance Event this weekend. On Friday there was Roger Sanchez in More, on Saturday I went with the girls, Ramon and those guys from The Hague, you remember, from Ibiza, to a party at Powerzone, really fantastic. Sunday I felt like shit, because at six in the morning we went to an after-party in town and the guys from The Hague slept at mine and, well, you can guess. We were so far gone that . . .

I delete the email.

From: Ramon_del_estrecho@gmail.com
Sent: 4 November 2001
To: Danvandiepen@hotmail.com

Danny!

You wanker, how are you? What's it like there with all those bloody kangaroos? Christ, man, how long have you been away? When are you coming back? Look, I'll give you a call soon, I want to hear your horny stories about Australian women. Are you still on the same mobile number?

R.

From: Frank@strategicandcreativemarketingagencymiu.nl
Sent: 7 November 2001
To: Danvandiepen@hotmail.com
Subject: Freelancer and shares

Dan,

Two factual questions:

1. I've put a freelancer on Volkswagen. It's the guy who used to work as a strategy planner at BBDvW&R/Bernilvy. I'm very pleased with him, and so is the client. So I want to offer him a contract, but you have to give your agreement. Could you confirm that for me?

2. We'll have to think about what sort of shares you want. I could maybe ask our accountant to draw up a proposal.

Good luck.

Frank

Eighteen

WONGALING BEACH, POPULATION 120, it says on the sign.

There isn't a single pub to be seen, and the only difference between the women and the men here is that the men have beards.

I'm having another of those days when I can't look at a Sesame Street Memory Game or a slide. So this morning I carefully asked Luna if she's missing her little friends at the crèche.

'No,' she answered with horror. 'I like it here, with you.'

That's OK actually. After all those heart-warming expressions of support there's not much for me in Amsterdam, either. Rose seems to have vanished from the face of the earth, the emails from Frank and Maud were pretty direct, and I can barely cope with Anne's urge to be helpful in an email, let alone live. Here at least I can click her away. Ramon and Tasha and the whole coke brigade seem even more pitiful, and I don't even feel like a shag any more, so I'm better off without the Dollies as well. And they're probably better off without me. It's as if no one cares I'm not there. OK, well, maybe a few porn sites mailed me to ask if I fancied dropping in some time.

Well, they can suit themselves, back in Amsterdam.

For months they took advantage of me, my drink, my drugs, my money and my dick, and now it's suddenly 'best if I'm away for a while'.

Maybe I'll spend the rest of my life here in Wongaling Beach (population ~~120~~ 122). Luna'd love that. At least I'd make someone happy. Maybe I've had my chance. I've lost Carmen, lost Rose, lost myself. Game over, no replay. Sometimes I wish that was how it was. That there was a delete button on my life.

But Luna's with me. *And I'll take good care of your daughter.*

Nineteen

After only two months in Australia, Luna and I have settled in very nicely. I say 'g'day' rather than 'hello', and 'no worries' rather than 'we've been sitting here for half an hour and the people next to us were served ages ago for Chrissake'.

We're getting used to everyday life.

It isn't nice, it just *is*. The day consists of playing with Luna, making sure she has enough to eat and drink, washing, swimming, putting off for as long as possible the point at which Luna is allowed to listen to her Walkman, until she's so desperate for the thing that I have half an hour to myself to read a book or quickly check my Hotmail.

And meanwhile try and see a bit of Australia, now that we're here.

For example, we're keeping a list of all the animals we see. There are some pretty weird guys here. After all, who on earth came up with the idea of a kangaroo, an emu and an animal with a duck's bill? As a creator you'd have to have been bored to death, or else been at the magic mushrooms.

Our list includes strange birds such as the ketchup bird – a bird that, according to Luna, calls the word 'ketchup'; you can't strip children of illusions like that – and the quiffpigeon, a creature with a quiff that would have inspired a deep bow from Elvis himself.

The other animals we've only seen at the side of the road. Every mile or so there's a sign bearing the picture of the animal that you can run over on that stretch of highway. Kangaroos in particular seem to have a strange habit of coming straight at headlights. That makes a hell of a mess. Every day I've seen scraps of kangaroo along the roadside, but I've wisely kept from mentioning it to Luna. She's wild about kangaroos and, let's be honest, they are scrumptious.

Yesterday she had a little bit for the first time, she thought it was great.

I told her it was chicken.

Kangaroo meat is hip here. You're not a proper restaurant if you don't have it on the menu. At first I thought eating the national symbol was a bit perverse, but after all, the Dutch eat cheese, and there were times when loads of us devoured tulip-bulbs.

We don't do much apart from eating and looking at animals.

On Dunk Island, for example, a stone's throw from Mission Beach, there's supposed to be an artists' colony, a magnificent thirteen-kilometre walking track with superb island views and more than one hundred and fifty species of birds. At least that's according to *Lonely Planet*; I haven't had the chance to go there. Madame Luna didn't feel like going to see that attraction. She wanted to play with her cuddly toys. We got no further than the landing stage where we were to be dropped off in the early afternoon. When we got back onto the ferry for dry land, I heard the other excited passengers saying enthusiastically that the island was phenomenal.

We'll have to forget sightseeing for the time being.

That's why, on my initiative, we've become fanatical swimmers. In a few weeks we'll be at the Whitsunday Islands, from which you seem to be able to sail to the most magnificent spots for snorkelling in shallow water. With a pair of flippers and armbands on her arms, I think I might persuade Luna to enjoy a bit of fish-spotting. Last week I started teaching her breaststroke. Every day she gets a lesson of at least a quarter of an hour. Standing behind her, I hold her tightly by her feet and move them up and down, calling out, 'spread, stretch, frog-kick'. As soon as I let go of her, she stops swimming and stands up. If she can't do that, because it's too deep, she panics, in spite of the Winnie-the-Pooh rubber ring we've bought here. We've had seven lessons now. She manages passably well with her arms, but her legs hardly ever move.

The second educational project – we've got tons of time – is playing with other children. Luna's very shy about it, so I hold her hand whenever there are other children playing and introduce her as 'Luna from Holland who would like to play too'.

The first time, this week on the sands at Mission Beach, she was back on my towel within two minutes.

After that she wanted me to join in. Dan quickly became a hero among her playmates, because my Dutch bridges, dams and dykes were, from the point of view of architecture, design technology and hydraulics, far superior to the ones built by the Australian toddlers. Luna beamed and quickly gained more confidence. She herself began, like a good Dutchwoman, issuing commands to the other toddlers. In Dutch.

Just recently I haven't had to do anything as long as I stayed nearby. I pretend to sit reading, but actually I'm watching my daughter playing, and taking photographs on the sly. Anne and Carmen's mother have already been sent a parcel of them. I'd really like to send Rose an envelope of photographs, too, but I don't dare. I sent one to Natasha at MIU. Maybe Frank and Maud will get to see them, too. Above all I want them to see that we're OK.

For the first few weeks I checked the websites of the Paradiso and More to see what fantastic parties were on there, but now I sometimes don't even notice that it's the weekend.

I don't feel the need to have people around me here, either. Every now and again I fall into conversation with someone in a restaurant or on a campsite, but I haven't chatted to anyone for more than a quarter of an hour. I don't care where they come from or where they're going. For honesty's sake, I'd have to add that not a single pretty woman has crossed my path, because that's the litmus test. For the time being I don't miss women, I don't even miss sex. I haven't even pulled myself off while I've been here, although it wouldn't be that easy, not with Luna lying beside me in a bed that's four foot across.

I'll have to watch out that it doesn't start coagulating.

Twenty

We stuck it out in Mission Beach for a week. It wasn't even that much of an effort, given there's absolutely nothing to do there.

Today I want to drive all the way to Townsville, another few hundred kilometres to the south. I give Luna her car-sickness pills before breakfast to give them enough time to settle camper-proof in her body.

It works. The two hundred and fifty kilometres pass without a puke. Luna has woken up and doesn't once ask how long it'll take until we get there, although with the strict speed limits it's a drive of nearly four hours and there's nothing to see on the way. The landscape around us is as white as Santa Claus's beard. They should erect a statue to Anne and her fairy-tale cassette.

When we've listened to the cassette twice through, we spend the last half hour of the drive singing.

I sing at the top of my voice. '*On Kangaroo Island, where kangaroos run wild, a kangaroo father plays with his kangaroo child, all together now . . .*'*

---

*   Song lyric by Het Cocktail Trio (1961).

Twenty kilometres and two dead kangaroos further on, Luna knows the words off by heart.

Singing, we drive into Townsville.

As a reward for being so good on the long drive, before going to the campsite we go in search of a playground. As I drive the camper along the boulevard I see one in the strip of grass between the road and the beach. I park the camper and tell Luna she can play for as long as she likes.

Meanwhile I go and sit in the grass and, out of habit, take my mobile out of my pocket to see if there are any messages. Of course not. No one has rung or texted me since Rose flew to Amsterdam from Bangkok.

I toy with the idea of giving her a ring. I should be able to do that now that eight weeks have passed, it seems to me. Just hear how she is. I've proved I can leave her in peace. Even though my fingers twitch every now and again, I still haven't sent her an email.

I calculate what time it is in Holland at the moment. Morning. And what day is it? No idea. I have to ask another parent in the playground what day it is. Friday. I speed-dial the number, but cancel it before it gets through.

Three times I pick up my mobile and put it back down again.

What have I got to say to her? That the weather here is good, and the speed limit never goes up? Or the elevating news that I tugged myself off in the shower at the Hideaway Caravan Park in Mission Beach, to the photographs I took of her in our apartment on Koh Samui and, after weeks of abstinence, came so violently that I nearly fell out through the swing door? Or shall I give her an enthusiastic account of Carmen's appearance in Luna's dreams and a playlist of the radio stations here, particularly when Carmen's the DJ? 'No, we don't miss you at all, because Carmen's travelling with us.'

So I just tap in a babbling text saying I'm fine, and so's Luna, as long as we aren't sitting in or on something that moves, and that I hope that she's well in far-off, autumnal Amsterdam. I send our message.

Then I take a look every few minutes to see if I've missed an incoming text.

Just as I'm creeping on my hands and knees through a red plastic pipe in the playground maze, making growling noises as I chase after a screaming Luna, I hear the liberating beeps. I don't know how quickly I can get out of that hose.

> Glad you're so well. Shame about Luna.
> Do you still have a lot of driving to do?
> I had a few difficult weeks here, but it's
> OK now. I've arranged to have a bite to
> eat with Maud this evening. It was nice
> to hear from you, but I don't want you to
> text any more. X. PS: I'm proud of you,
> good Papa.

Life goes on in Amsterdam. Even Rose's life.

Twenty-one

I'm on the other side of the fucking world, worrying all night about how a woman who isn't my girlfriend is going to be spending her evening in Amsterdam.

Shall I just text her again to wish her a good time with Maud this evening? Luna is snoring beside me. What time is it in Holland?

Half past six in the evening.

What time will they have arranged to meet? Maud works till about six, then of course she'll want to have a good old moan for a bit, so about eight, I reckon. Where would they actually go?

Rose and Maud. They haven't been all that close over the past few months. Maud was quietly jealous of Rose because she could see how much I meant to her, and in turn Rose wasn't all that fond of Maud. She probably also knows by know that we weren't playing the Sesame Street Memory Game on Ameland, given Frank's violent reaction.

But they might be able to become good friends now that I'm at a safe distance. They're both from Breda, they both like nice food and neither of them feels at home among the sleekly designed Dollies in Natasha's club.

I have the feeling things are going to get out of hand with those two tonight. They'll be drinking over dinner, and you can be sure that they'll swap secrets, because that's the way women are. Before you know it, each will have told the other exactly how, where and in what I did it with each of them, and they'll suddenly understand sooooo well why each of them did what they did with me, before hugging and kissing each other with a screech of laughter, raising their glasses to one another and swearing that they're both going to take the first moderately decent bloke they see home with them and shag him senseless.

The sluts.

Do you want to bet that by the time they roll into the Pils-vogel or the Bastille, they'll be willing prey for all the randy sods walking round in there?

I don't give a damn what Maud does, she can get herself pulled apart for all I care, but my stomach turns at the idea of Rose having sex with someone else.

Ten past three.

In Amsterdam it's now, let me think, just turned seven. Rose will be doing herself up. Dressed to kill, because she knows that Maud is no slouch in the clothing and make-up department. She'll have so much cleavage on display she'll need to put red lights on them to get safely down the street.

Rose will probably be wearing that little black skirt with the square-cut blouse. Really tarty. And those black boots. Or the pink high-heeled mules.

Of course! I can safely wish them a lovely evening together. Then I can see if Maud's still cross with me.

What's to stop me? Aren't I just being considerate?

> **Have a lovely time tonight with Rose. I'm glad you're going out together. Where are you off to? Everything great here! X**

That's one.

> **Have a lovely time tonight, Goddess. Watch out for unsuitable men.**

Five minutes pass and I don't hear anything. I did send it, didn't I? Shall I just – no, I saw the little sent-message envelope.

Eight minutes. Damn. What business is it of mine?

■

Still nothing. That's more than ten minutes.

■

Did I calculate correctly, is it really evening in Holland? Let's just check. Australian time minus eight hours. Yes, that's right.

Unless my message to Rose misfired.

Twenty-two

Day breaks slowly. I've been lying brooding for two hours now. Has Maud revealed that we nearly always slept together on Monday evenings after the Dinner Club? Why haven't I been honest and admitted to Rose that I had sex with so many other women apart from her that, from time to time, I didn't know what was happening?

I know why. Pure cowardice. I knew that even though we weren't 'together' she'd never have accepted it, and I didn't want to hurt or lose her. And losing the only other woman I'd felt happy with in only a few short months was something I'd wanted to avoid.

I made no room for scruples in the months after Carmen's death. I didn't brood or restrain myself, not for anything or anyone. Deep down I felt it would be an insult to Carmen if I suddenly started being faithful to Rose, who wasn't even my girlfriend. No, but the only regrets I ever had during that time involved Rose. She was the first woman I was unfaithful with, in the sense that I felt something for her. A situation I'd always wanted to avoid.

Perhaps my promiscuous behaviour after Carmen's death was even a weird form of revenge. Like I – in some weird twisted logic – blamed Rose for my betrayal of Carmen. Jeez!

Twenty-three

'Pap, what are we going to do today?'

Wait till Rose has woken up and ring her, find out why I still haven't heard a damned thing and everything they got up to last night . . .

'Hey, shall we find out what sort of things there are to do here?'

I take the *Lonely Planet* out of the little cupboard over the sofa bed and see what I've circled on the Townsville pages. What a surprise! 'Would you like to go and look at fishies?' I lift her onto my lap. 'There's a great big aquarium near here.'

She looks at me blankly.

'A great big fish-bowl. You can look into it.'

She nods. Plan ratified. Now to the less easily digestible part of the day's schedule: 'And later Papa has to go to an Internet cafe for a moment. I have to send a couple of emails.'

Questioning eyes.

'Send some messages to Grandma and Anne and Thomas. Tell them we're fine.'

'And Rose?'

'Erm – perhaps her too, yes. And then you can listen to your Walkman for a little while, OK?'

She nods. 'And then will we go back to the playground from yesterday?'

■

At the campsite I hire a bicycle from Koala Bike Hire, a little shop which to Luna's great delight has a koala as its logo. There's one on every helmet. At the camper I throw our swimming gear into a rucksack, put the helmet meant for me in the cabin of the camper and pedal to Great Barrier Reef Wonderland.

The woman at the till, who reminds me of a beached sperm whale, hands us our tickets. We enter a big hall with a globe hanging from the ceiling. I walk up to the globe and show Luna where Holland and Australia are. She throws her arms around the thing and can just touch both countries. The photograph I take of it will go down well in Amsterdam.

We arrive at a glass tunnel with sharks, rays, giant turtles and another impressive fish swimming above it. I've seen lots of things from below in Amsterdam, but never a shark or a giant turtle, let alone a humphead Maori wrasse.

Luna anxiously stays right in the middle of the tunnel, at a suitable distance from the glass, following open-mouthed the sharks swimming above her as if in a slow-motion game of tennis. Her hand is tightly clamped to mine.

Finally we see the clownfish live. Luna thinks he's very funny, but the seals are her favourites today. She can't be dragged away from their pool.

Every now and again I glance at my mobile to check that Rose still hasn't sent me any news of herself.

At the end of the tour Luna is allowed to choose between

a cuddly seal and a clownfish. She opts for the seal. Or for the clownfish. Or rather the seal.

With a furry seal and furry clownfish under my arm we walk outside. Things are going to be cramped in bed tonight.

When we reach the playground on our bike, Luna starts crowing. I can't work out what's so special about the slide, the climbing frame and this seesaw here. I guess it has something to do with the fact that the place is familiar after yesterday. Children are just like old people: why move house if there's nothing wrong with this one? As far as Luna's concerned, we could skip the rest of Australia. She runs to the slide that she went down about three hundred times yesterday, and I go and lie in the grass. And peer at my phone again.

Still no text.

Twelve o'clock. Four o'clock in the morning in Amsterdam. Jesus, shouldn't she be home by now? Or is she asleep already?

Suit yourself, I'll risk it.

> Hi Goddess, lying here by a playground on a boulevard in tropical Townsville, just seen sharks and clownfish in Reef aquarium, brilliant. Later a comprehensive account by email, I'll go to the Internet cafe this afternoon. How was this evening? If you're asleep already I'll hear/ read it tomorrow. X.

My heart pounds in my throat as I press 'send'. What a lot of words to ask what I want to know. Whether there's anyone in bed with her. Remind me never to become a writer.

A minute later my phone beeps.

> Just home. Was veyr enjuyoable. Mme
> Jeannette, Pilsvogel, club more. Bedtime
> now. I'm trying to get you out of my head.
> Give me a chance.

Yes, and what happened in Club More? Hello? What am I supposed to do with that kind of information? She's clearly drunk as a skunk. And is there someone with her? No, she wouldn't write 'bedtime now'. Although, in passing like that, in the middle of the text – that's how I'd do it.

■

Beeep. Beeeeep.

Ah! So she isn't shagging yet.

> Oh, I snet you a long email this atfernoon.

I feel my throat tightening. A long email.

Where's there an Internet cafe around here?

I pick up the *Lonely Planet* and open it up on the page marked by the Great Barrier Reef Wonderland pamphlet. I'd already circled it. Just near here.

Where's Luna? On the slide.

'Luna!'

She waves.

I gesture to her to come over.

She shakes her head, slides down the thing and runs back to the steps.

I stand up out of the grass and walk over to her. 'Shall we get going?'

The corners of her mouth turn downwards. 'But we've only just got here . . .'

'Yes, but today we've got to, erm – we've got lots and lots of things to do . . .'

'Like what?'

'Go to the cafe where Papa has to send emails. And I'm hungry, surely you are, too?'

'No,' she says with a shake of her head. 'I'd rather go on playing.'

She runs back, this time to the climbing frame, where I spent a quarter of an hour negotiating yesterday, too, before she finally agreed to come with me.

Now I know that Rose has sent me an email, my head's completely in Amsterdam, as much as it was when my body was there, too.

Something tells me this can't be her intention.

Shame, then. I want to know what she wrote.

'Just a minute, then, love,' I call. Luna pretends she doesn't hear me.

Damn it, we've been here for nearly an hour. At every playground we've been to she's almost immediately started whingeing at me to push the swing or catch her at the bottom of the slide, and now she's waving and smiling at me as if she plans not to budge from here for several days.

I stand up and walk towards the slide.

'Luna, we're going.'

'Where to?'

Sigh. 'To get something to eat.'

'Are we coming back here later on?'

'No, after we've had lunch we'll go to a cafe where Papa can send emails, you remember?'

She lowers her head and stamps on the grass. 'I want to stay here.'

'No, Luna! We're going to eat now.'

I get to my feet and hold out my hand.

She slaps it away. 'No-ho-ho-ho!'

Parents and children are beginning to look in our direction. I throw them my best everything-under-control smile.

'Luna, we're going. Come on.'

She starts stamping harder. And crying. I start feeling like a fool.

'Luna, I'm going to count to three.'

She starts crying even harder.

'One . . .'

The crying turns into screaming.

'Two . . .'

She shakes her head like one possessed.

'Three!'

I grab her hard by an arm. She tries to lie down on the grass. Christ almighty, if it weren't for all these people standing staring at us, I'd thump her on the spot.

I furiously pull her with me. She screams hysterically as I drag her behind me along the grass like a doll. Finally we get to the bikes.

I take her face between my fingers. 'Are you going to bloody well behave yourself now?!' I scream into her face.

'No!!!' she screams back.

I turn her over roughly and slap her on the bum.

She gives a sudden start and glares at me.

'I – I – I wa – aa – ant to – hoo go – ho to *Mama*.'

For a moment the words paralyse my body, as if the world around me has suddenly frozen.

'You can't go to Mama!' I hear myself yelling. The parents and children around us are watching with mounting amazement. I couldn't give a stuff any more. 'Mama is completely fucking dead!' They'll be able to hear that in Sydney. 'Mama is dead – I'm your Papa and there's nothing I can do about it.' I slump on the ground next to Luna and start crying along with her.

She comes cautiously over on her knees and sits down next to me.

We sit on the ground like that for a while. Luna stares at me, perplexed, wiping her tears from her cheeks with one hand, rubbing her bottom with the other.

I hold her head tightly and stroke her hair.

'I'm sorry I hit you.' I give her a kiss.

She shrugs, creeps over to me and lays her head against my shoulder.

I start sobbing again. Very quietly, stroking her cheeks.

We lie like that for several minutes.

'Shall we go and get something to eat at McDonald's?' I ask.

Twenty-four

McDonald's survives on guilty parents.

We order far too much.

'Do you want chips, too?'

Luna shakes her head and noisily sucks a drop of her half-litre of orange juice, staring over my shoulder, apparently at something interesting. I turn round and follow her eye. There's a little boy sitting eating behind us. He's wearing a T-shirt with a cartoon of a construction worker on it.

'That little boy's got a Bob the Builder T-shirt,' says Luna.

'He's wild about Bob the Builder,' I suddenly hear a woman saying behind me, in my own language. I look round, right into the eyes of a laughing blonde woman. Well, makes a difference from that sperm whale at the till of Great Barrier Reef Wonderland.

'Luna loves Bob the Builder too, don't you?' I reply.

Luna shakes her head. 'No, I don't.'

The woman bursts out laughing. What lips . . .

I laugh and shrug. 'Normally she does everything I say, you know,' I grin.

'I saw you yesterday at the playground,' the woman says in English-accented Dutch. Am I glad she didn't see me there today. She's wearing a V-necked T-shirt.

'Are you travelling with your daughter?'

'Yes,' I say stoutly. 'First in Thailand and now here. We're heading south. What about you?'

She laughs, baring her teeth, and points to the lad in the Bob the Builder T-shirt. 'We live here.'

Suddenly Rose is very far away.

I hold out my hand.

'Hi. Dan. Nice to be able to talk to someone in Dutch about something other than playgrounds and clownfish.'

She laughs and introduces herself as Tanja. I see that Tanja isn't wearing a wedding ring.

She catches me looking.

'I'm divorced.'

'Ah,' I say. 'That creates a bond.'

'You too?'

'Yes. Blamelessly divorced.'

That laugh again. She looks at Luna and her son, who are hovering shyly around each other. 'My son doesn't speak Dutch all that well. He does understand it, though. We mostly speak English at home. My ex is Australian.'

'If you like, you two could go and play in the playroom for a minute,' I say to Luna, pushing her gently in the back. 'Perhaps . . .'

'Ben.'

'Perhaps Ben would enjoy that too . . .'

Luna looks at the little boy and asks if he would like to. Tanja explains to her son what Luna just said, and sits down at my table.

We talk about what there is to do here in Townsville apart from the Great Barrier Reef Wonderland (bugger all), what she does for a living (yawn), and all the places in Queensland Luna and I have been to already (babbledy-babble, oh what a brilliant dad I am). Within ten minutes I've got her phone number, and we've been invited to dinner at theirs this evening. I reply that we'd be delighted, write down her address and then walk with her, chatting cheerfully, towards the children, where I tell Luna the happy news that she and Ben are going to see each other again this evening because we're going to eat at Auntie Tanja's.

Whistling, I ride my Koala Bike Hire bike, with a properly helmeted Luna on the back, towards the Internet cafe.

Shagging tonight.

Twenty-five

From: Roseverschueren@campaignresults.nl
Sent: 22 November 2001
To: Danvandiepen@hotmail.com

Dear Dan

A few weeks ago we were still together in Thailand, now you're in Australia and I'm in Amsterdam.

This is your trip. I've felt that from the moment I was naive enough to go with you to Thailand. I didn't belong there. In fact I had already stopped belonging when Carmen died. You wanted less, I wanted more. Unlike all those other girls, I couldn't share you (though I don't know who you slept with and how often – I wouldn't be surprised to hear from Maud tonight that you went to bed with her far more often than you care to admit).

In spite of all the criticism from the outside world, I'm happy with what we had together. Perhaps I should feel humiliated, because I tried to wrench myself in so many different directions for our love, but at any rate I did everything I could to give it a chance, in spite of the walls that you constantly erected after Carmen's death.

To feel your constant resistance to me, to the growth of something that could have become real love, as if it were all horrible, was so painful that it practically killed me.[*]

You told me once that just after Carmen was diagnosed with cancer, you looked jealously at an elderly pair giggling together in the supermarket and realized you would never do that with Carmen.

But there's a double game going on. You yearn for just such an intense and long-lasting love, but left to your own devices, life just becomes a sequence of novelties, of lucky breaks.

Sneaky, temporary affairs, flings, one-night stands: they're exciting, thrilling, hot and ego-stroking. But you're turning them into a lifestyle, a lifestyle that means you're always play-acting.

I don't think a double life can ever lead to real love. You end up always busy hiding who you really are from the one who loves you. Perhaps I could have somehow learned to cope with your infidelity, just as Carmen hoped. Fidelity isn't a goal in my life. Fidelity is a means to achieve goals. I think if you love someone, you've got to do everything you can to make that person happy. If I was convinced monogamy made you unhappy, then perhaps, if I'd been absolutely sure of your love, I might have joined you in looking for a form of relationship with which both of us would have been happy.

But I have to accept I haven't been able to bring out the Dan who dares to give his heart. And I don't want to live with a different Dan. The Dan who dares to give his heart exists, everyone's seen that.

---

[*]   This sentence, along with the theory of opening phases, is based on one in a letter from Leslie to her boyfriend Richard in *The Bridge Across Forever: A Love Story*, a wonderful book by Richard Bach. Well worth the trouble. You've got to love writers who sit firmly in the chairoplane.

Carmen was incredibly happy during her last weeks. I hope that someone else, perhaps even – my heart almost shatters at the thought – someone in Australia, will manage to meet that Dan again.

I've decided not to phone or text you any more. For my own sake, and for yours. Later on, when you're back, I want to stay friends, on one absolute condition, a condition that you promised me when we had our first conversation. Our friendship will be platonic.

Dan, you're having a good time in Australia. I love you.

X, Rose

PS: In Bangkok I slipped a little present for Luna into your rucksack, in the bottom section. A new *Jip en Janneke* book. After two months she's probably sick of her other reading books.

PPS: Nice picture of that Dolly in your rucksack. I didn't know sheep could shear themselves.

Twenty-six

'Have you got that much fanmail?' I hear a voice behind me. I think I sense a little irritation. 'The food's actually on the table.'

Oh, stop, will you. Let me come down to earth for a moment.

'Umm – yeah – I'm coming.' I look at my watch and see that I've been reading for three-quarters of an hour now. 'I had a lot of emails,' I call in the direction of the kitchen.

The other emails I've received – Thomas, Carmen's mother and a selection of porn offers – I haven't even opened yet.

'Have you got a printer, erm – Tanja?'

'Under the computer,' she calls from the kitchen.

The Internet cafe wasn't a great success this afternoon. No sooner had I opened my Hotmail than Luna had taken off her Walkman and was standing next to me.

'I have to wee.'

Off to the toilet.

'I'm bored.'

New tape in the Walkman.

'I'm cold.'

My sarong around her shoulders.

'I'm so tiiiiiired . . .'

I was too excited before my date to get cross, even though I still hadn't read a single letter of Rose's email. Where had I left that telephone number? Oh yes. In my trouser pocket.

'Hello?'

'Tanja?'

'Yes?'

'This is Dan. Could I use the Internet at your house for a bit this evening, before we go and eat?'

Great woman, that Tanja. Internet + eating + drinking + playmate with matching Dutch-language video for Luna + 99.99% chance of sex for Papa.

And all for free.

Now I've got a plate of pasta with tiger prawns in front of me, and three printed A4 sheets of *Rose Writes to Cancel* beside me in my bag. I hope the pasta's more digestible.

Tanja chatters away cheerfully, about her divorce and about Ben's school. I'm as absent as Liam Gallagher at an Oasis gig. The only thing I do, on automatic pilot, is pour my third glass of Chardonnay in a quarter of an hour ('I got this bottle from my mother when I got divorced from Jerry, to be drunk for a special treat . . .') and try to nod, shake my head and say 'yeah!' at the right time.

Tanja doesn't care. She's clearly happy for the chance to spit bile about her ex-husband in Dutch. Complaining in your mother-tongue is just the best.

Luna is having a great time, too. She's sitting on the floor with Ben, watching a Dutch video of Bob the Builder. She's barely touched her hamburger and chips.

Every so often scraps of Rose's email flit through my

head. *Constant resistance to me. Sequence of novelties. Lifestyle that means you're always playac—*

'Are the prawns nice?'

'Oh – erm – yes. Definitely. Delicious.'

'Good. Listen, there was one thing he always insisted on: he wanted me to talk to Ben only in English, and every time he saw Ben he would ask the poor child if we really did speak only English at home, and then if he found out that it wasn't the case he stopped his alimony or threatened to take Ben away from me, when he can't even look after himself properly . . .'

Tanja's story interests me even less than a score in the Dutch second division. Why don't I just go back to the camper when I've thrown the last prawn down my gullet? It's easily done, if I've got Luna with me. A daughter's bedtime is the perfect alibi for an early interruption of the evening.

I watch her carrying the plates into the kitchen. Nice arse.

'Coffee?' she calls.

'Please.' I guess she won't talk so much when she's shagging.

She goes on clattering in the kitchen. Now that she can't see me, all I have to do is listen.

Instead I surreptitiously take from my bag the sheets of paper with Rose's email on them.

You yearn for just such an intense and long-lasting love, but left to your own devices, life just becomes a sequence of novelties, of lucky breaks.

I hear something coming chattering, and quickly stuff the A4s away. I manage a vague smile.

'So. Coffee.'

233

'Yes. Delicious.'

'Anything in it?'

'No. Black.'

'At least that's cheap,' she says with a laugh. I thought only Anne and Thomas said that sort of thing.

'I think it's nice that you're here, you know. Jerry never liked just sitting at home and chatting.'

I'm beginning to see Jerry's point of view. He was a wise man to get the hell out.

'Shall we go and sit on the sofa?'

Oh my!

I sit down a safe distance away from her.

With my coffee in my hand, I look around the room.

'Nice house you've got.'

'I've done it all up. When Jerry . . .' – My God, what am I doing here? Have I really escaped all the way to Australia to have myself nagged at for three whole – '. . . and then I thought, that's it, get rid of everything that reminds me of that bastard . . .' – hours in a house with a through-lounge in Townsville, the Maarssen of Queensland, just so that I can stick my dick into some divorced chatterbox's fanny? – '. . . and I completely repainted the bedroom, and decorated it with my own things . . .' It's as if Rose is laughing at me ten thousand miles away.

'Shall I quickly show you the bedroom?'

OK. An open invitation. She winks as she says it, too. Does she imagine I'm going to get my leg over while my daughter's sitting downstairs? Bloody hell, we're not in Amsterdam . . .

Luna's yawn comes right on time.

'I'm afraid my daughter's getting tired,' I say apologetically, with a nod to my daughter. Go on yawning, darling, yawn away.

'She can just as easily sleep here, you know, I'll put an extra mattress in Ben's room.'

Tanja's hand slides towards my leg. My whole software system is programmed to throw an arm round her now. Don't do it. Don't do it. I look at Luna. Help me, sweetie. Ask if we're going home. Start crying. Do something.

Her hand strokes the top of my leg. It feels like an iguana's creeping over it.

'N . . .'

'Come on,' says Tanja. She taps me playfully on the thigh and pulls me towards the stairs. 'I'm just showing Uncle Dan the house, Ben.'

Twenty-seven

I lie on my side looking at her. The morning light peeps in through a chink in the curtains and plays with her blonde hair. She stretches and yawns. I smile.

How beautiful she is.

She slowly wakes up. She blinks and laughs at me.

I bend over and give her a kiss on the forehead.

'Good morning, my little ray of sunshine . . .'

'Hi, Papa . . .'

'Are you glad we came home?'

She nods. 'I didn't think there was enough room to sleep there.'

'Neither did Papa,' I grin, 'although I didn't dare say so to the lady.'

'You didn't?' she asks, surprised.

'No. But I thought it was much nicer to sleep with you in the camper.'

■

An hour later I've paid the bill for two nights on the campsite with my credit card and loaded everything into the camper, and we're driving away from Townsville, before Tanja and Ben get the idea of coming to see us with a pot of fresh coffee and breakfast that I expect she calculatedly bought in yesterday.

I look over at the driver's seat. Luna is sitting flicking through Rose's *Jip and Janneke* book.

I lay my hand on hers and smile.

Papa and Luna in Australia.

I'm so glad Luna saved me. While Tanja was showing me her room with all her own things, and from force of habit I was about to grab hold of her and push my tongue towards her tonsils, I heard Luna's panicky voice downstairs.

'Papa, where are you?'

And wham! I was back with both feet on the ground.

Ten minutes later we were politely thanking Tanja for a delicious dinner, the Internet and the Bob the Builder video, and agreeing we'd give them a quick call today to tell them what time we might have a barbecue at our camper this evening.

And now we're driving towards Bowen, another few hundred kilometres to the south.

Nickelback thunders out of the speakers, and on my instructions Luna learns to headbang.

'*Never made it as a wise man … This is how you remind me of what I really am …*'

See you and thanks, olé, olé.*

---

*   Wrampled from the B-side of NAC. [Breda football team supporters]

Twenty-eight

It's been three days now since we left Townsville and Tanja's clutches.

Tanja rang another five times or so, left two cross messages on my voicemail and then fell silent. You can't run away from an omelette without breaking eggs.

We're sitting in the Harbour Lights Caravan Park with – how surprising – a playground and a swimming pool. Luna's over the moon. There's bugger all else to do in Bowen, and that's all to the good, because I'm finding myself quite enough to be going on with at the moment.

On the way here from Townsville I was still pleased with what Rose had written. I even sent her back a thank-you text. It looks as if she's keeping her word, and it hurts more than I'd expected.

While I'm pushing the swing, while Luna's digging in the sandpit or while she's asleep, Rose's email is still prowling around my head. Now and then her sentences force their way into my consciousness:

> You yearn for just such an intense and long-lasting love, but left to your own devices, life just becomes a sequence of novelties, of lucky breaks.

Evening after evening I sit by my camper thinking. It's been blown out of proportion, I always thought, this infidelity stuff. Once home from a quick shag, I was the ideal husband. I'd want to prove my escapades didn't interfere with my true love for Carmen. So it was like I had to win her back, with little presents, dreaming up nice things to do together, and having lots of sex – at home, too – so she wouldn't get wise to me. I did it for the same reasons – to escape the boredom of life – that I was mad on parachute-jumping. It's just a sly little hobby of mine.

Hmm, escapades, the word says it all: it's no more than an innocent form of escapism, half the world's unfaithful. The closer you look, the more men make a habit of hanky-panky. For the average Frenchman, Italian, Greek, Brazilian, Surinamese and West Indian, being unfaithful's like having a crap: everyone does it and nobody talks about it. Eyes shut and voices silent. I reckon Ramon's got it absolutely right: half the men who say they're never unfaithful are lying, and most of the others are too ugly to get the chance. According to Ramon, one in ten men are monogamous for their whole life out of principle, out of love.

Take guys like Thomas. At home he's the good family man, but as soon as he's free of wife-and-mother, he gets, as he puts it, 'his finger wet'.

And women are complete hypocrites.

Ramon and I could spot them a mile off when we ran into them in Rhodes or Majorca, the ones who were up for it. Married women on holiday on their own, women whose husbands no longer saw them as women. With three well-timed compliments you can slip in there like a knife through horny butter. And their husbands just think that darling wifey went on holiday to read the latest Danielle Steel.

Even I spent years in the naive belief that my own Carmen was as dependable as the Bank of Switzerland. Her best friends didn't even know that she'd been unfaithful a few times. Women have the knack of being unfaithful discreetly.

Not me.

That was what hurt Carmen the most, she told me during her last weeks: that for years she hadn't known what half of Amsterdam knew. Rose says the same thing, in fact.

I don't think a double life can ever lead to real love. You end up always busy hiding who you really are from the one who loves you.

I never wanted to hurt Carmen. I don't want to hurt anyone, certainly not 'The Woman Who Is Going to Change My Life', if I ever meet her. What I once managed, just by chance, to do with Tanja in Townsville, thanks to Luna, I won't find quite so easy when I'm back in the Amsterdam sweet-barrel. I love the excitement of a different body, breasts I've never touched before, the idea of a new, thrilling pussy. I really don't want to spend my whole life having sex with one woman.

The idea that I have to stay faithful feels like a handbrake on my life.

It can't be the meaning of love.

Twenty-nine

When I bought the *Lonely Planet* guide to Queensland in Amsterdam, I still thought I was coming here to see a bit of Australia. In my travel guide there are big fat exclamation marks by the Whitsundays, a group of islands that are supposed to be a paradise. We're at the Island Gateway Holiday Resort in Airlie Beach, the village that's the setting-off point for the Whitsundays. But the name of the campsite seems utterly cynical, because even here Luna and I can't get much further than the booking agencies. The short sailing trip round the Whitsundays lasts three whole days. I can't inflict that on my daughter. She'd have puked herself inside out halfway through day one.

To my surprise, I notice that I'm finding it easier and easier to put up with it. We've gone into the village a few times this week. That was nice, too.

In Airlie Beach, for the first time in Australia, I came across something that was relatively sociable. There's an artificial lagoon where people flirt and sunbathe, and the main street is full of restaurants and cafes. Unlike the rest of Queensland, they don't have a problem with me bringing Luna along.

That my tips are generous is beyond dispute,[*] and you can't say the same of the other tourists. Because Airlie is the Khao San Road of Queensland. Everywhere you look there are backpackers, most of them just a few years older than Luna. And twenty years younger than me. Here, father with child stands not for strong & sexy, but for old & past it.

I'm struck by all the twenty-year-olds who seem to be living in another world. I don't feel the slightest impulse to talk to them.

The peace does me good. I haven't wept over Carmen since Townsville. Although I haven't heard from her since Cairns, it feels as if she's still there. More and more often I'm thinking of cancer-free Carmen and the lovely things we used to do together before she fell ill.

Luna's enjoying herself, too. My state of mind clearly exudes a calm that keeps her in a good mood.

It could also be that I'm making fewer demands of her.

In the morning I spend a couple of hours with her in the swimming pool, showing the patience of an angel, and since I worked out that I did something wrong in my breaststroke lesson – her leg stroke looked so daft – things are getting better by the day. The tactic of stopping the lesson as soon as she loses interest is starting to bear fruit. I'd never thought of that before. After four days she can swim across the pool all by herself, with a rubber ring around her waist. As a reward, and out of healthy self-interest, I've secretly bought her two armbands at the camping shop at the Gateway Resort. Perhaps then we could go swimming together

---

[*]   Wrample from *The Shadow of the Wind*, Carlos Ruiz Zafón (2004).

in the sea at Fraser Island in a week or two. She'll get them then.

Because of the voluntary boundary that we've placed on our radius of activity, we spend the whole day walking around barefoot. I haven't worn my trainers once. Very rarely, if I have to go to the toilet, I put slippers on, but I really don't have to, you've got more of a chance of catching athlete's foot back home than here at the campsite, because Australia is very clean. No one even dares to crap next to the pot, as European folklore claims. No one pinches towels from the washing line, no one leaves a mess at the many barbecues scattered around all the campsites. Australians have respect for each other, for each other's things and for nature. They're not that wild about immigrants, but Luna and I don't count, because we're blond.

I'm coming to like the Australian Way of Life. The excessive friendliness, the ultra-decency, the *no worries, mate* even makes me less cynical.

Every day we take a stroll through the woods that line the campsite, and go in search of animals that haven't yet appeared on our list of 'Animals We've Seen'. Meanwhile Luna has a whole folder of photographs of insects, birds and other animals that you'd have to go to the library to see in Holland. We still haven't spotted any koalas or (live) kangaroos, but today's big hit was a real kookaburra. It was gone before I could catch it on camera, but I drew it, and Luna thought that was great, too.

Even if they're dead, animals are our best friends. Luna and I have discovered the barbie. After a few days I'd had enough of the restaurants on the main street. Now every day I buy a chunk of meat in the campsite shop and in the evening chuck it on one of the many barbecues they have dotted round the place. Luna thinks it's fantastic. She can play in the grass until it's nearly ready, and she doesn't have to wait nicely until a waiter decides to bring her a fish finger or a sausage. She's clearly impressed by my grilling technique. In her eyes I'm Jamie Oliver. Open-mouthed, she watches me char a lamb with one hand, while I carbonize a couple of sausages for her with the other. When she's not looking, I quickly scrape off the most disturbing black bits, throw on a daub of cocktail sauce and Bob's your uncle.

I'm starting to appreciate the camper, our private rabbit hutch on wheels, more and more. Precisely because it's so small we're never inside it. Camping, which I've always really disliked, now gives us a bit of a rhythm. I'm starting to see the charm of the daily activities we carry out together as much as possible. Luna is visibly proud when she can make herself useful.

'We're very busy, aren't we, Pap?' she said this morning as we were filling the water-tank before doing the washing up.

■

Now she's having a nap. I'm washing the clothes. That's necessary, because I have no clean underpants and Poppy's starting to whiff, as I noticed when Luna parked the thing about two inches away from my face in her sleep last night.

I'm standing comfortably in the laundry room folding Luna's knickers and T-shirts. I can't remember ever doing that at home, but it feels very Zen.

After that it's Luna's doll's turn. Bending over, I scrub the thing clean in a vat of soap-suds. If it had been my doll I'd have thrown it away ages ago and bought a new one. Now I think of the prospect of Luna happily pressing it to her face tonight and falling contentedly asleep with her thumb in her mouth.

Maybe love isn't as complicated as I thought.

Thirty

'*You know your love ... is liftin' me ... liftin' me ... higher and higher.*'

With my right hand I copy a singing mouth, my miming fingers facing Luna and myself in turn. My daughter is shrieking with laughter in the passenger seat. I turn Jackie Wilson a bit louder and sing exaggeratedly along.

'*That's why your love ... keep on liftin' me ... higher and –* FUCK!'

A flashing light.

The red letters in my rear-view mirror leave little doubt that the warning sign is meant for me.

STOP ... STOP ... STOP, it flashes in bigger and bigger letters. I quickly put on my seatbelt and turn the music down.

'What are you doing, Pap?'

'We've got to stop for a minute, sweetie.'

I gradually slow down and pull up on the verge.

We're on a road with cornfields on either side. I haven't seen another car for miles. Where this police car has come from is a mystery to me.

In my mirror I see two cops getting out. One of them looks at my number-plate and says something into a walkie-talkie attached to his shirt. The other one slowly walks towards our camper.

I wind my window down.

'G'day, officer.'

'Why weren't you wearing your seatbelt, sir?'

'Wasn't I?'

'No, sir. And you were driving at one hundred and thirty-eight kilometres per hour.'

'Was I?'

'Yes. We have a one hundred kilometre per hour speed limit.'

'Well, we were singing and –' I can see by the policeman's face that this explanation isn't adequate. The argument that I'd quickened the pace considerably because we had to travel six hundred kilometres today to reach Hervey Bay presumably won't cut much ice.

'Can you step out of the vehicle, sir?'

'What are you doing, Pap?'

'Pap has to get out of the car for a minute, lovey.'

Luna looks anxiously at the policeman. I put on a reassuring expression and get out.

The policeman gestures to me to stand against the car. He searches me thoroughly. It's like the Paradiso.

He asks me for my driving licence and flicks through it. Cairns Airport Revisited.

'Are you aware that exceeding the speed limit by more than twenty kilometres is a crime under Queensland law, sir?'

Queensland law. Not that again.

The policeman tells me to wait there for a minute. He walks back towards the camper and takes out a ticket-book.

One way or another I have a feeling I'm going to have to hand over more than a bag of lollipops this time.

■

'How much did you say?'

'Two hundred and twenty-five dollars for not wearing your seatbelt and three hundred and fifty dollars for exceeding the speed limit by more than thirty kilometres per hour, sir.'

Like emptying a bucket.

'Cash.'

'Excuse me?'

'You have to pay your fine here and now, sir.'

You can't be serious. I burst out laughing.

Five hundred and seventy-five dollars.

The cop isn't laughing along. I quickly make a serious face.

'But that's ridiculous! I haven't got that much money with me.'

'If you can't pay the fine, I'm afraid you'll have to leave your vehicle here, sir.'

'What are you doing, Pap?' Luna asks again, this time in a piping little voice.

I look around. Cornfields as far as I can see.

And a burning sun.

I have a problem.

Thirty-one

We're standing at the side of the road with our rucksacks and a receipt that says we can collect the car in Hervey Bay in a few days in return for payment of five hundred and seventy-five Australian dollars. Luna's lower lip starts to tremble as the policeman sits down in the driver's seat of our dinky toy. I feel humiliated. It's like having to watch as someone shags my wife.

We slowly see our dear little camper-van disappearing out of sight. The police car drives proudly behind it, as if it had just captured a prisoner of war.

'ARSEFUCKBOLLOCKSING QUEENSLAND!' I SHOUT. I kick my rucksack.

'What a naughty policeman, huh, Pap?' Luna adds. She gives the rucksack a little kick as well.

It actually makes me laugh.

And what does it all matter. I lift Luna up and swing her around. 'Shall we have a look and see if they have any ice-creams in here?'

She nods violently.

We skip into the filling station.

Shortly afterwards we're sitting against our rucksacks in the sun, licking two iced lollies.

■

We'd nearly been left in the middle of nowhere, but the cop with the mobile phone clearly thought that was a bit harsh, given the make-up of our team. So we were allowed to drive the camper to the nearest filling station ourselves, and phone for a taxi from there.

I decide to wait till we get a lift from someone who stops to fill up their car. With Luna beside me I look very trustworthy.

Thirty-two

With the second vehicle that comes along we get a bite.

A truck with a gleaming red bonnet and big chrome pipes. The driver, a man with a belly that's clearly been constructed with the help of tins of Fosters, listens to my story and shakes his head. The Queensland police often do that to tourists.

'No worries, mate.'

The driver has to get his cargo to Brisbane, a few hundred kilometres south of Hervey Bay, and could use some company along the way.

I run to our rucksacks, throw them into the cabin and then lift up my daughter. Luna looks terrified. Compared with our own camper-van, this truck's an aeroplane. We're almost two metres above the road.

The driver isn't wearing a belt, I notice. And there's barely any room between his belly and the steering wheel. Luckily there aren't many bumps in Highway One.

Luna's eyes pop out of her head at the sight of the cabin. On the dashboard, on the ceiling and behind our seats there are huge quantities of flowers. It's like the Botanical Gardens in here.

The truck driver sees Luna looking. 'One for each time I return home safely.' He gets the flowers from his daughter, he says, pointing to a photo-frame on the dashboard. His eyes twinkle.

He babbles away about his daughter and, with his enormous hands, takes a drawing she made for him out of the glove compartment. He asks me if Luna can draw as well as that.

Two hours later we're at the entrance to the camper-van park in Hervey Bay. Without a camper, but with a plastic flower and a great big smile.

Thirty-three

The camper-van park still has lots of holiday cabins free, a kind of camper without wheels. Low season has its advantages, too.

Luna's asleep and I'm sitting peacefully with a beer outside our holiday cabin. Tomorrow we're taking the boat to Fraser Island.

Losing the camper hasn't been too bad so far. We'd already planned to go to Fraser Island, and you aren't allowed to take cars there. The five hundred and seventy-five dollars is basically nothing more than a rather pricy parking fee.

This campsite's practically deserted, too. A few plots further away there's a camper that I saw two young girls getting out of this morning. One of them was gorgeous. I gave her a friendly nod on the way to the toilets and left it at that.

I can't help grinning. In Amsterdam now I'd probably have been sitting with Dolly XXXCVIII in De Pilsvogel or Vak Zuid, wondering whether I should take her along to More or the Paradiso for form's sake, or whether I should just drag her home to bed.

I never knew it could be so comforting not to see every woman as a walking potential shag.

Thirty-four

Australians are just children, really.

A delicious breakfast is a 'yummy brekky'. A barbecue is a 'barbie'. A bottle of beer is a 'stubby'. And if you've overindulged on them, you just phone into work next day and take a 'sickie'. It's like the country was founded not by the British, but the Teletubbies.

They don't just talk like children, they *are* just big children. On Fraser Island, for example, they've set aside the whole of the eastern coast, a hundred kilometres, so that they can go charging about on 4x4s.

I can imagine that. So, to my surprise, can Luna, when I explain that we're allowed to drive cars along the beach here. After our bicycle ride along the beach at Port Douglas, she loves the idea of us doing that together.

The man hiring out the 4x4s has other ideas as soon as he sees Luna. I see the same expression in his eyes as that time with shark-tooth guy at the diving school in Port Douglas. I tell him I'm not going to let my daughter do the driving, but he's not to be moved. 'Too dangerous with kiddies, mate.'

I shrug, and so we spend the next day reviving the Captain Nemo Experience: Luna and I and a whole swarm of elderly tourists and budget backpackers travel along the beach in a bus. A bit like a tram-ride, but with all-terrain tyres and camouflage paint to make it seem a bit more exciting. Every now and again we're overtaken by beeping 4x4 jeeps and Land Rovers full of whooping people in their thirties.

The bus drops us off near a wooden board with the words **LAKE WABBY 4.3KM** on it. Half of the old people don't bother, and flop down on the beach. A smartly dressed New Zealander and his wife are up for the walk, they say. They have a girl of about fifteen with them. She's their youngest daughter, he tells me. An afterthought. Their oldest daughter was already studying when the youngest was born.

I say nothing. If I ever meet 'The Woman Who Is Going to Change My Life', Luna will get at best a little half-sister or half-brother. If it ever happens, I'll just let Luna say brother and sister, I decide.

Their youngest daughter is a great success, I say. The New Zealanders beam with pride. Two German backpackers, too young to know that Holland was a lot better in 1974, clearly agree with me. They stroll along the dune path beside the girl, about fifty metres ahead of us. The adolescent mating dance.

After a few hundred metres Luna's had enough of walking. I put a little sun-hat on her, put her on my shoulders and walk along with the father and his wife. It's more than thirty degrees and the sand is powdery. I'm sweating like a pig.

'Carrying your little daughter through the desert, that must feel good,' says the wife.

'Couldn't feel better,' I pant back.

They laugh. Where am I from, and am I here alone with my daughter? I tell them my wife has died. The woman gives a start and says she's very sorry.

I say with a laugh that I can cope with it by now. To my amazement I mean it, too. Over the past two months I've become more emotionally stable, I notice.

We've been talking for half an hour now, longer than I've talked to anyone since Tanja. Every now and again I ask if Luna's comfortable on my shoulders, and if she wants another drink. I feel pretty good like that, I must admit. I ask the man if he'll take a photograph of me and Luna. Father and child in the desert. The man says it'll be a brilliant picture.

Another kilometre and a half, I would say. In front of us one of the two German boys puts his arm around the New Zealand girl. He hasn't worked out that he's being spied on. He tickles the girl in places where I haven't had my hand in weeks. She giggles affectedly and runs a little way ahead. Soon all three are over the top of the dune. The father quickens his pace slightly. He murmurs that you never know with boys these days. His wife replies that he himself was exploding with lust in the old days. The man looks at her with surprise and bursts out laughing. He starts tickling her in the same way as he just saw the backpacker doing. She giggles and tries to tickle him back, but he takes her arm and kisses her. I hang back a little bit until I'm walking about ten metres behind them.

The image of the backpacker's fizzing hormones does nothing to me, but I am touched by the love between this man and woman.

I get the same feeling as I had with that elderly couple in the Albert Heijn supermarket. Enthralled, I look at their linked hands, a few metres ahead of me on the top of the dune. I try to imagine how they met, what their life together was like when they were thirty. They were probably just as happy as Carmen and I were at the start. Except that they've been forty and fifty together, and later, as is only fitting, sixty, seventy and perhaps even eighty.

My thoughts are interrupted by shouts of joy. Lake Wabby must be on the other side of the dune. It's time. I'm almost collapsing with the strain. Luna asks if the water over there is the lake. I tell her that if it isn't the lake then I don't know what it is. Right in front of us, surrounded on three sides by high sand dunes and on one by forest, is a magnificent, greenish-blue lake. The German boys and the girl are already lying in the water, whooping exuberantly.

I lift Luna down off my shoulders.

'We're going swimming, sweetie!'

She looks at the water. 'Will I be able to put my feet on the ground?' she asks in a frightened voice.

I take the new armbands out of my bag. There are dolphins on them. That should give her confidence. The first dolphin to drown has yet to be born. Luna isn't convinced. She looks back at the lake. This is a long way from the swimming pools on the campsites where we've been bathing so far.

I kneel down and look her right in the eyes.

'Papa will hold you tight,' I say.

She looks alternately at the armbands, the lake, and then back at me.

'Really?'

'I promise.'

A minute later we're lying together in the water. Two metres away from the side it's already too deep to stand up.

'Do hold on tight!' Luna quavers anxiously.

'I'll hold you tight.'

With one hand under her belly we swim away from the side. I feel that Luna has enough support from the armbands, but don't let her go for a second. We slowly swim to the middle of the lake.

'Take a look around,' I say when we're further away from the side than anyone else.

She turns around and sees with surprise where we are. Her eyes begin to glitter.

'I can swim, I can swim, Pap!' she crows. She slaps the water with her arms.

Suddenly the last thing that Nora said to me, almost three months ago, darts through my head.

Your daughter gives you much more than you think.

Thirty-five

In the days after Lake Wabby we do a lot of hiking with the New Zealanders. We bump into each other on the beach of the artificial lagoon and eat together a few times, in the buffet restaurant at the resort. Meanwhile their daughter has been won over by the German boys and eats at their table every evening.

I tell the couple about Carmen, about the reasons why I'm here and about my affair with Rose.

One evening when his wife, like Luna, goes to bed early, I invite the man to come and have another beer outside my apartment.

When I open my second bottle, I tell him how jealous I'd been of him and his wife this week. I ask if they were always so happy together.

'Well, I was,' he says with a grin, 'but she wasn't.'

He tells me that on the campus where they'd met as students, he was well known as a womanizer. When he and his wife married a few years later, they made an arrangement with one another. 'I said to my wife: darling, you want monogamy? Marry a swan,'* he says with a laugh. 'And then she came out with the Sex Commandments.'

No calculated sex. No regular mistresses. No love. No affairs. I nod sympathetically.

And last but not least, he says: tell each other everything with complete honesty. Always. 'Every single fuck.'

I'm flabbergasted. Why? I ask him. Why hurt the other person when it's just about sex?

He shakes his head. 'That was the only way for us. She knew I would never be faithful. That was the only way she would never have had to wonder whether I'd had sex with another woman when I went away for a weekend with friends, or if I came back from a business trip.'

I pick at the label of my bottle of Fosters. 'And,' I ask after a while, 'did it work?'

He looks at me and explodes with laughter. 'No. Not at all.'

He explains that everything was fine at first. His wife understood that men can separate sex and love. Before they had children, she had had a few sporadic flings as well. But after the birth of their first two children it got harder, and she felt less need for free love. He continued unabated.

'And then it went wrong,' he says, almost guiltily. He noticed that her emotional limits were reached much more quickly over the years.

He started hushing things up, to avoid hurting her. She started suspecting him, because she felt that something wasn't working. She started checking his things, his shirt-collars.

---

* Wrample from *Heartburn* (1986), when Meryl Streep's father explains to her why hubby Jack Nicholson has been unfaithful.

She rang his office to see if he was there when he'd phoned earlier in the day to say he had to work late.

It couldn't go on: she trapped him. She had noticed that when he rang to say he was driving away from his last client, he was always home exactly three-quarters of an hour later. She had taken a map of the area where they lived and phoned all the motels three-quarters of an hour from their home. Eventually she got a bite. Mr So and So had indeed checked in. She picked her two children up off the floor, sat them in the car and drove like the devil to the motel in question. When he was about to check out, along with a blonde, just to take the shine off things, she plonked their two children down on the counter in the lobby and said she wished him the best of luck with his new family.

He tells the story with a mixture of admiration and shame.

I'm lying across the table with laughter. What a story! What an amazing woman!

After a year's cooling-off period, he continues, they went to relationship therapy together, twice a week, for more than a year.

'It was hell on earth, mate.'

Slowly they came back together again.

He picks another bottle of Fosters up from the table. I can see from his face that he's getting emotional. Without a word I hand him the opener.

Why didn't they get divorced? I ask him after a long silence. Why did she want to stay with him, and he – in the two tough years that followed – with her?

I see his eyes welling up.

'We love each other, mate.'

Thirty-six

Sorry for texting you after all. I'm in bed, a bit tipsy and emotional. Just had a touching and impressive conversation with a New Zealander. Couldn't help thinking of you. Have a great Christmas. Where are you celebrating? X.

Thirty-seven

The New Zealanders leave the next day. They want to go home next week to celebrate Christmas.

Suddenly Fraser Island feels different. Now that my first friends in months are gone, I've had enough here. We can collect the camper from the police station near Hervey Bay, and I think that's what we're going to do. I miss the thing. At reception in the complex I pay the bill for the nights we've spent there and Luna and I take the first boat back to Hervey Bay.

The camper feels like coming home. I leave the police station almost six hundred dollars lighter. By way of punishment I hold my horn down for several seconds and then pull off at full speed from the car park.

Keeping strictly to the speed limit, we drive via Gympie (which always looks nice in photographs) to Noosa, a little town famous for its starred restaurants. It's less than a hundred kilometres to the south, by Australian standards hardly worth starting the engine for. On the way we see the plumes of smoke that the papers here are full of. But say what they like about the bush fires, the smoke smells delicious. Very pleasant, so close to Christmas.

Munna Point Caravan Park is already in Christmas mood.

There are Father Christmas hats on the lamp-posts, and they've sprayed fake snow on the windows of the reception hut. It's thirty-four degrees.

The camper park is on a little beach along the Noosa, a river that flows into the sea. People are surfing in the distance. Here, by the campsite beach on the river, are the families with children. And pelicans that have come in search of snacks. Luna can't get enough of them, and I shoot a whole roll of my daughter giving the big birds bread.

It's dark by the time we think of getting a bite to eat ourselves. I decide, since we're in Noosa, to eat a hole in my credit card. We go to Le Monde, apparently the place to be.

I order *soupe de poissons, un plat du jour* and *du poulet et des frites* and have the waiter bring a bottle of the best Chardonnay from the region and a colouring pad with felt-tip pens for Luna. Even though there are European newspapers laid out on the table, I read Rose's email for the umpteenth time. After hearing my New Zealand friend's story, the email reads like a piece of inescapable logic.

I was, Rose writes, always busier hiding my double life than letting love come into full bloom.

As I scoop up my soup, I think about it. She might be on to something. My double life was a time-bomb under my relationships, even under my relationship with Carmen. Deep inside I knew it could never go well.

The main courses arrive. I ask Luna to push her colouring pad aside to make way for the plate of chicken and chips.

I peel a scampi, stick it in my mouth and point to Luna's plate of *poulet et des frites*. Luna looks at it and says she isn't hungry.

Why on earth don't they disguise the creatures the way they do at McDonald's, with a layer of breadcrumbs?

The children's menu in Le Monde cost more than a day's camper rental.

But Luna starts whining and says she wants to go back to the camper.

'Papa saw on the menu that they have reeeeally delicious ice-creams for children!' I try. And crème brûlée and good espresso.

I ask the waiter to hurry up with the desserts.

Less than five minutes later I have to give up. 'I'm so tiiiiiiiiired . . .' wails Luna.

Seconds away from my crème brûlée I ask for the bill.

Outside I call a taxi and pull Luna towards me on the back seat. She snuggles into me. Before we get to the camper park she falls asleep.

Thirty-eight

When Luna was a baby I slept like I was in an ice-hockey tournament: in three short chunks. By day I faced up to nappies that would have been banned under the Geneva Convention on chemical weapons.

Now Luna is three and a half, and from the day we first set foot in the country she has managed to mess up everything that makes Australia a nice place to be. Diving on the Reef, toad races in Port Douglas, 4x4 rallying on Fraser Island, crème brûlée in Noosa: with Luna there, you haven't a hope.

If a woman had pulled all those stunts on me, I'd have dumped her ages ago.

With Luna, it's never occurred to me to give up on her. I've never questioned for a second whether I love her. I've never thought I could be happier without her. OK, there was a moment at that diving club in Port Douglas.

With a woman I'd have given up long since.

Every crisis, every row, every moment of boredom and every rubbish day I ever had in a relationship made me wonder if I really loved the woman. Was this really the one I wanted to grow old with? Mightn't there be a woman who was easier in terms of everyday life?

When I met Carmen, I had the feeling for the first time

she might be the one, the long-awaited love of my life. I was happy, everything worked. I loved her to pieces. I was scared stiff the happiness granted me would one day be taken away. That Carmen would put me out with the bins because she was fed up with me. Or she had someone else. Or found out about one of my flings.

That's what happened. Carmen found out I'd slept with Sharon, the receptionist at BBDvW&R/Bernilvy, the ad office where I was working at the time. Then she knew for sure I could never be faithful, or even try to be. Years later she told me that after the Sharon episode she'd been on the point of leaving me, but she loved me too much.

And that's where I went wrong.

Rather than being less unfaithful, or even giving it up completely, I convinced myself I had monophobia: fear of a monogamous life, the consequence of which was a compulsive need to be unfaithful.

Now, ten years later, I'm starting to understand what it was that really frightened me.

I was scared stiff of love.

For the first time in my life a woman had me in her power. I was so afraid of losing Carmen that I myself took the initiative and, bit by bit, chipped away at what we had by having as many flings with other women as possible. And after that I just had to wait for the final blow.

Where that bloke from New Zealand stopped and gave himself and his wife the chance to surrender to love, I would have gone on running until everything fell apart. I've begun to realize that if Carmen had stayed healthy, I myself would have run away, because my relationship with her 'didn't mean anything any more'. And so on to the next disaster.

Strange as it may sound, in the end I should be grateful for the cancer.

What I mean is that, ironically, I think that while the cancer killed Carmen, it saved our love.

'*You remember how great it felt to look after Carmen during her final weeks?*' Nora said. '*Luna can teach you how great it is to love someone again.*'

Nora was right.

If I stay scared of love, then I'll have to admit, in thirty or forty years' time, those two weeks by Carmen's deathbed were the happiest time in my life.

Then Carmen really will have died for nothing.

Thirty-nine

After yesterday's culinary debacle, Luna's allowed to choose what we're going to do.

'Cycling, Pap, like that time on the beach!'

I hire a bike from reception at the Munna Point Caravan Park and ask the woman behind the counter where we can cycle along the beach in Noosa. She looks at me with surprise. The pride of the town is a ten-kilometre-long cycling promenade, magnificently laid out, right through the marinas, across lakes and canals and along the bay.

That's fine too, I reply hastily. As soon as the sand's in view, we'll take a look.

We get a map and cycle along the wooden cycling promenade to Noosa Beach. Watched by a surfing class of *Baywatch*-worthy girls, I lift my bike down the steps and on to the beach.

Within three metres I'm stuck. This isn't cycling sand.

I hear the girls laughing. With some difficulty I convince Luna this isn't a good idea. I quickly dismount.

To my delight, there's a selection of French, Italian, Greek and Australian haute cuisine on the beach. Luna's allowed to choose the establishment.

With two hot dogs and enough ketchup and mustard to

bring you out in teenage spots, we go back and sit on the beach. Luna's eyes gleam. She presses up against me, we digest our hot dogs together and laugh at the *Baywatch* girls, most of whom, to my great satisfaction, end up flat on their faces in the water rather than standing on their boards. That'll teach them.

As we cycle along Hastings Street, the local equivalent of P.C. Hooftstraat, I see, among the designer stores, a souvenir shop with a window display of artificial Christmas trees.

■

'Luna, what do you think of the idea of a Christmas tree in the camper?

She sits up and starts bouncing in her seat.

I lift her from the bicycle and lock it. Meanwhile Luna runs to the shop and presses her nose against the window.

As well as Christmas trees there are dolls.

I see her looking at a cloth doll with yellow-blonde hair, in a turquoise dress with a heart on it. The doll has a big embroidered smile. A cheerful character, by the look of it.

When I'm paying for the Christmas tree, a few Christmas decorations for inside the camper and two Father Christmas hats, I add the doll, taking care that Luna doesn't see.

■

As soon as we've reached the camper I tell Luna I've got a surprise for her. I hand her the gift-wrapped parcel.

Luna throws her arms around me when she sees what it is.

I beam. Easy goal, this one.

'You know what I'm going to call her, Pap?'

'Claudia Schiffer?'

'No, I'll call her Rose.'

I give a start. As far as I can remember, since Thailand I've avoided talking about Rose when Luna was there. I already feel guilty when I think of her as I'm reading *Jip en Janneke*.

'Erm – Rose. OK. Why Rose?'

She shrugs. 'She looks like Rose.'

I look at the doll's laughing mouth and blonde hair.

She hasn't even got tits, I want to protest, but I keep my mouth shut.

Luna grabs her Rose and gives her a cuddle.

Does Luna.

Forty

The outskirts of Brisbane look like one of those mining towns you always see in British films where the head of the family has a belly, a bulldog tattoo and an alcohol addiction.

I look around to see if I can find an Internet cafe anywhere.

I see one at a crossroads. A bright-yellow building with a shop window on which it says in big red letters that an hour on the Internet only costs fifty cents. Let's go for it.

I park the camper by the side of the road. After a tough negotiation, Luna and I agree that I can have one hour ('until the big hand's gone all the way round') in the Internet cafe. Armed with Poppy I, Poppy II, Rose-doll and a few other cuddly toys we go in.

I've heard nothing from Rose since that email in Townsville.

I've had no reply to the text I sent after the conversation with the New Zealand guy. I plan to email her about Luna's new doll, but only if I've had an email from her.

Heart thumping, I log on to Hotmail. My eyes slip feverishly along the names in my in-box.

The selection is even more disappointing than the mail that Thomas has sent me, with the title 'Ajax-PSV 1–3 :-)'

No sign of Rose.

I scroll down. Nothing there. There's only her notorious email from three weeks ago.

What a bummer.

Why are women always so resolute when it doesn't matter? Disappointed, I open the other messages in my in-box. Carmen's mother sends me a Christmas card; there's another email from Thomas, this time with a blurred little film of a black woman; Frank asks if I'll be back before 31 December to answer the question about my shares, and tells me at the same time that his new strategist is also interested in taking part of them over from me. Newsletters from Club More and Arena and the weekly offers from Bol.com. Nothing. Niks. *Nada* from Rose.

My stomach clenches.

'Luna, we're going.'

She has arranged her Rose right in the middle of the circle of the other cuddly toys on the floor of the Internet cafe. So it's her birthday.

I still have another forty-seven minutes left, I see on the screen. I look at the Ajax site for a moment to see how Ajax are going to lose this weekend, and see on www.nos.nl that there's going to be a speed-skating tour in Holland. Fascinating.

But let's log back into Hotmail for a minute. She might just have – no.

Disappointed, I log out.

'Luna, come on, we're going.'

'But you said we were going to stay here until the big hand's gone all the way around . . .'

'Clear up those dolls!'

She sadly starts throwing her dolls into her Winnie-the-Pooh suitcase. 'And you should write and tell Rose that I've got a doll called Rose.'

'You just mind your dolls for now, OK?'

■

Newmarket Gardens Caravan Park is three blocks away. We drive into the car park. I don't like the look of it. The reception hut looks just as dilapidated as the suburb in which it stands. The barrier is up. I decide to take a quick drive around. What a let-down. There isn't a single person in the whole Newmarket Gardens Caravan Park.

We are, you might say, alone.

I drive back to the entrance. There I look at the decrepit reception building. There's a sign saying OPEN. It doesn't exactly radiate conviviality. There isn't even any fake snow on the windows. And this is where we're supposed to celebrate Christmas? I glance at Luna. She's listening to her fairy-tale cassette.

I take the map. The table says that the distance between Brisbane and Byron Bay is one hundred and eighty kilometres. Including this horrible bit to the north of the centre of Brisbane perhaps one hundred and ninety. Two hours' drive. That way Luna will get some sleep. Perfect timing. Just perfect for her midday nap.

I give Luna a pill and a sweet, start the engine, leave the Newmarket Gardens Caravan Park and set my course for Australia's number-one-love-and-peace spot.

Forty-one

BYRON BAY 189 KM

This is your trip, I've felt that from the moment I was naive enough to go with you to Thailand. I didn't belong there.

Thailand was a self-fulfilling prophecy. I was looking for confirmation there would never be anything between me and Rose, and I received it. It was empirically proven: we weren't meant for each other. Full stop.

BYRON BAY 157 KM

In fact I had already stopped belonging when Carmen died.

She's right. From the day Carmen died our relationship hadn't a hope.

Of course. She was the only one I didn't need to drink myself stupid to be with. She was the only one with whom sex didn't feel empty, the only one with whom I didn't mind if she just wanted to stay asleep.

I felt at home with Rose. But it was hopeless.

Rose was part of the past, and if there was anything I didn't want after Carmen's death, it was the past. It was summer, the future had started again, and Amsterdam was at my feet. I really didn't want her to be 'The Woman Who Is Going to Change My Life'. Rose was yesterday's papers.

BYRON BAY 132 KM

. . . at any rate I did everything I could to give it a chance, in spite of the walls that you constantly erected after Carmen's death.

Whenever we threatened to get anywhere close to something like a relationship, as we did after our wonderful weekends in Antwerp and Rotterdam, I thought up reasons why it couldn't work, or did things that meant it really wouldn't work.

BYRON BAY 111 KM

Unlike all those other girls, I couldn't share you (though I don't know who you slept with and how often).

I shagged a whole flock of young sheep. It was my way of stamping out any spark of love, which terrified me.

BYRON BAY 61 KM

Your constant resistance to me, to the growth of something that could have become real love.

But I really didn't want love, God damn it! I had two weeks to test it, and then love was dead, dead as a doornail. I hated everything and everyone capable of evoking a feeling that threatened to come anywhere close to love.

Fuck love!

BYRON BAY 38 KM

In spite of all the criticism from the outside world, I'm happy with what we had together.

After Carmen's death I was even more ashamed to be seen with her than before. I wanted to avoid the merest hint that anything could have developed between me and the woman I'd betrayed Carmen with.

BYRON BAY 23 KM

I have to accept that I haven't been able to bring out the Dan who dares to give his heart.

I didn't want to love you.
I wouldn't let myself.
I wanted to fuck your love away, so there you have it.

**WELCOME TO BYRON BAY
CITY OF LOVE AND PEACE**

■

I wake Luna. Her dummy is still in her mouth, Rose-doll in her lap. I take one hand off the steering wheel and stroke my daughter's hair.

'Sweetie, we're there.'

Forty-two

The dazzling white of the lighthouse of Byron Bay hurts my eyes. The air is cloudless, and there is nothing but ocean as far as the eye can see. There's no one else here. Near the lighthouses there's a sign saying that this is the easternmost point of Australia. You have to have something to be proud of.

I turn round and touch the door of the lighthouse. It's open. I go inside and climb the spiral staircase. Heart thumping, I reach the top. I step outside, on to the circular platform.

The view is breathtaking. I lean over the railing and stare at the sea, the magnificent, calm blue sea far below me. I throw my head back, shut my eyes and listen to the soft swish of the waves. What peace, what refreshing peace.

All of a sudden the steel door of the lighthouse opens. Shit! Am I actually allowed in here? Australia is a negative version of Amsterdam: you're not allowed to do anything until you've had explicit permission. My heart pounds in my throat. A woman in a blue dress appears in the doorway. I shield my eyes with my hand.

An overwhelming sense of happiness washes through me. A smile appears on my face. I want to cry out.

The woman in the blue dress smiles her broad smile, the left-hand corner of her mouth curling the way only the left-hand corner of her mouth can curl.

'Carmen!'

Carmen, the same radiant, glorious Carmen I know from before the cancer. She blazes with health and her smile is just as mischievous as it was then, as though at any moment she could come and sit on your lap with a view to shagging you.

Sadly she doesn't do that.

Instead she strokes my hair. I fall into her arms and rub my head against her shoulders like a little boy. She frees herself from my grip, takes my hand in hers and guides me to the railing.

In the distance, in the middle of the sea, I see a dot that's gradually getting bigger. I shield my eyes with my hand and stare towards the water. As the dot gets closer I see that it's a little boat. Not all that surprising in itself, for a moving object on the sea. I squint and see a silhouette.

The little boat slowly comes closer. The contours of the silhouette become clearer. It's a woman. With blonde hair. My jaw drops.

Rose is in the boat.

Amazed, I turn my head towards Carmen. And back to Rose. And back to Carmen. I want to say something, but Carmen puts her finger to my mouth, smiles and just nods.

I carefully climb on to the lighthouse railing. I look round once more.

And then I go and stand on the railing, look at the little boat bobbing in the sea below, close my eyes, spread my arms and, the sweat of fear on my forehead, I jump.

Forty-three

When I wake up, tears are flowing down my cheeks.

Luna sees them and gently strokes my face.

'Papa, are you sad?'

I smile though my tears.

'No. As a matter of fact I'm very happy. And there's something I want to talk to you about.'

Forty-four

'Hello?'

'Erm – hello . . .'

For a few seconds there's silence. 'Dan. Isn't it?'

'Yes – Hi. It's Dan. Can I, erm – can I talk to you for a second?'

Silence.

I hear a sigh. 'Go on, then.'

'OK . . .'

'How – um – where are you calling from?'

'A phone box in Byron Bay.'

'Where's that?'

'A few hundred kilometres north of Sydney.'

'And – is it nice there?'

'Yeah – it's a bit like the beach at Bloemendaal, but warmer, less crowded, more relaxed, a lot of surfers, some great food, nice people . . .'

'Hey. Sounds pretty good.'

'Yeah, not too bad.'

'Oh.'

'Would you rather I hung up?'

'Oh – I don't know.' I hear Rose blowing her nose. 'I

didn't like it when you kept texting me. But at the same time it's nice to hear you for a moment.'

'How – how are things?'

'Shit.' She can't help laughing through her sniffles. 'But you're well, yeah?'

'We are, aren't we, Luna?'

Luna nods enthusiastically. She looks at me expectantly. 'We're doing a lot of nice things together, we're seeing all kinds of things together, we quarrel together and laugh together, and when Luna's asleep, then – then I think.'

'Go on . . .'

'About myself, about me and Luna, about Carmen, about love . . .'

'Have you – have you met someone there?'

'More or less.'

'Oh.'

'And you?'

'No, of course not.' She sounds irritated.

'What are you doing for Christmas?'

'I don't know yet,' she says with a deep sigh. 'I might go to my mother's. I haven't made any plans yet.'

Luna is tapping my shoulder more and more urgently.

'OK, then.' Three, two, one, *jump* . . .

'Do you fancy coming out and celebrating Christmas in Byron Bay?'

'Pardon?'

'We – I – want you to come to Australia.' Luna sits up and starts nodding violently. 'And I have a sense Luna agrees.'

'. . .'

'Rose?'

'. . .'

'Rose?'

'Wha – but – wh – why?'

'Because I've worked out that I . . .'

'That you what? . . .'

'That I love you.'

Forty-five

We're an hour and a half early.

I've been spinning out the time all day. The ball-boys at Ajax have nothing on me. First, before we got into the camper in Byron Bay, we visited an Internet cafe to see if her flight had been delayed. Then we lay on the beach at Surfers Paradise, spent as long as we could eating at Burger King, used up our daily portion of playground, and then went into another Internet cafe near the beach to see if her flight had been delayed. I was spared that at least, because I really couldn't have spun out the time for much longer.

She's landed, the screen above our heads tells us. Right on time.

A small miracle, given that she had three stops on the way. There wasn't a single airline with a free seat so close to Christmas. My threat that my new girlfriend had to be here for Christmas, if I had to hijack a plane myself, gave the girl behind the desk at the travel agency in Byron Bay an idea: there's an Islamic airline, Royal Brunei Airways, that flies via London to Brisbane. Admittedly with stops in Dubai and Brunei and, OK, we would have to book an extra flight from Amsterdam to London as well, but then it would all be all right.

All in all she was travelling for forty hours. She'll get a special Christmas present for that.

It seems like an eternity since yesterday morning, when I read Luna the text in which Rose said that she was just boarding the plane at Schiphol. Since then I've been pointing to a map of the world every hour or so, showing where Rose probably is at that moment. I'm even counting the hours since I rang her, four days ago now.

When we set off from Byron Bay in the camper this afternoon, heading back towards Brisbane, I felt like I used to on a Saturday evening when I was finally able to jump on my bike to the NAC stadium at Beatrixstraat in Breda after dinner.

In my excitement over Rose's arrival I clean forgot to give Luna her tablets, but my daughter was in such a good mood that her body spontaneously forgot to be car-sick. I found a radio station playing dance music, and as I drove I showed Luna how they dance to it in Ibiza. She was over the moon.

When 'Another Chance' by Roger Sanchez came on, I practically blew the speakers. The last time I heard that song I was lying in the pool in Ibiza staring right up the fanny of one of the Dollies. I immediately swap that image for the prospect of the moment when I take Rose in my arms.

It hadn't taken her long to make a decision. I'd told her how I'd spent the past few months. The constant depression of the first month. The impact of her email that evening with Tanja. The conversation with the New Zealander. The rediscovery of love, simply by feeling how much I loved Luna. The drive to Byron Bay and my realization that I'd done to her what I had done to Carmen: fucked my love away for fear of that same love.

'And do you trust love now?' Rose had asked.

'If you really want to know: it scares me shitless . . .'

'Then I'll come and help you,' Rose said resolutely, after a conversation lasting forty-three minutes and eighteen seconds.

Holding Luna in my arms, I had gone and jumped up and down on the grass beside the camper.

Since then I'd been floating. My aura burned a hole in the ozone layer, my power of attraction seemed suddenly to have soared to the level of George Clooney and Father Christmas squared. Children smiled at me, barmen thought I was just the best guy in the world, the most gorgeous women in Byron Bay winked and flirted, but I was unprecedentedly unapproachable.

The only one I was thinking about was Rose. We lay there all day texting each other. I did it from the beach at Byron Bay, she from shops in a wintry Amsterdam, desperately looking for bikinis, summer dresses and flip-flops.

In my openness I had – as soon as I'd got hold of a ticket for Rose – emailed the home front. I had a new girlfriend, I wrote. She was on her way from Holland to Australia now, and she'd be travelling with us from Christmas onwards. And her name is – Rose.

No one shared my enthusiasm.

I hadn't received much mail for the last few months, but now that changed.

Thomas and Anne thought it was all a bit soon, six months after Carmen's death. 'Don't expect to be welcomed with open arms,' Anne emailed. Maud said it hurt. Ramon thought I had a tendency to press buttons wildly when things were going against me, and he suspected that was happening again this time. 'Why Rose all of a sudden?' wrote one of the Dollies. Natasha mailed to say that she didn't understand why, after three months in Thailand, I suddenly loved Rose. Carmen's mother said Carmen would probably have been pleased for us, and she was thinking of trying something similar herself. Only Frank didn't respond.

I hadn't made any friends by taking Rose to Thailand on the sly. Or by openly inviting her to Australia.

■

The first passengers come through the doors. Luna is jumping up and down, forever asking where Rose is. I'm even more nervous than my daughter. It feels as if she's suddenly walking into our lives.

Luna sees her first. She tugs on my arm and points.

'Papa, look, Rose, there!' she whispers shyly.

There she is, between the sliding doors of Brisbane Airport, looking around for us.

The future has started again.

Acknowledgements

907 of the 58,638 words in this novel are demonstrably not by me. That's about one and a half per cent, or more precisely 1.55% for the statisticians among you.

147 words (0.25%) come from other writers. Written samples, or 'wramples'. If you can do it in music, you should be able to do it in literature, too. In the footnotes you'll find out precisely which words and expressions I've borrowed. The most important: 48 words come from Richard Bach (from *The Bridge Across Forever*), 47 from Carlos Ruiz Zafón (from *The Shadow of the Wind*), 27 from Yann Martel (from *The Life of Pi*), 13 from Jacob van Duijn (from *Hyper*) and 12 from Jan Wolkers (from *Turkish Delight*).

435 words – 0.74% of *The Widower* – come from song lyrics. About twenty fragments have been incorporated, by artists including Tröckener Kecks (92 words), Peter Koelewijn (62), Snow Patrol (24), Doe Maar (19), Nickelback (16), Het Cocktail Trio (14), Moby (7), Roger Sanchez (6), Jackie Wilson (5), the Troggs (100), Fun Lovin' Criminals (64) and the B-side of NAC (5).

Finally, about 491 words, or a good 0.84% of *The Widower*, are based on stories, anecdotes, remarks and expressions by friends. These 491 words are distributed as follows: 231 from an anecdote told to me by Chris, 123 from a story of Jaan's, 62 from a blunder by Bien, 23 from a legendary remark by Femke, 17 from an observation once heard by Rena, 16 made by Tom, 13 from a sentence that my nephew Bart once heard someone say and two expressions of 3 words each come from Engin and Kurt. And then, doubtless, there are also words, anecdotes from people I've met in or at Project X, de Pilsvogel, Ibiza, Thailand or Australia.

A lot of wisdom, expressions and rituals about coke and the use of coke are inspired by Ad Fransen's book *Coke* (2005).

■

Dan's analysis of infidelity and married women as a target group was previously published in *Red*. Some sentences about the Ibiza club scene appeared in *Nieuwe Revu*.

I've transposed the Old Dutch Acid Party and the concert by Tröckener Kecks in the Vondelpark to a different point in time.

Thanks

I wish to thank the editors Janneke and Harminke, who once again ruthlessly went to work with their red pencils.

My co-readers Don, Elly, Heidi, Kurt, Marni, Mars and Naat for all the energy they put into their comments on my manuscript.

My unimaginably erudite publisher Joost Nijsen for his trust and wisdom.

Mars, Marco, Hugo and Eric for all the marketing they have done on these 58,638 words.

Dory, who advised me to jump.

My wife Naat for everything she does and my daughters Rose and Eva for giving me the chance to write whatever and whenever I like.

Visit **www.panmacmillan.com** to read more about all our books and to buy them. You will also find features, author interviews and news of any author events, and you can sign up for e-newsletters so that you're always first to hear about our new releases.

www.panmacmillan.com

GIFT SELECTOR
YOUR ACCOUNT
WISH LIST
WAITING LIST

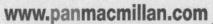
HOME | ABOUT US | IMPRINTS | TRADE/MEDIA | CONTACT US | ADVANCED SEARCH | SEARCH | GO

BOOK CATEGORIES | WHAT'S NEW | AUTHORS/ILLUSTRATORS | BESTSELLERS | READING GROUPS

Coming Soon...

Reading Groups

Competitions
Feeling Lucky?

Extracts
Sneak Previews

Interviews

Events
Meet Our Stars

Reviews
What The Critics Say

News & Awards

Editor's Choice
What We're Reading